Tales of the Bark Lodges

Books by Bertrand N. O. Walker
(Hen-Toh)

Tales of the Bark Lodges by Hen-Toh, Wyandot
Yon-doo-shah-we-ah (Nubbins) by Hen-Toh, Wyandot

Tales of the Bark Lodges

By Bertrand N. O. Walker
(Hen-Toh)

With an introduction by
Daniel F. Littlefield, Jr., and James W. Parins

Banner Books
University Press of Mississippi / Jackson

First published in 1919 by Harlow Publishing Company
Introduction copyright © 1995 by the
University Press of Mississippi
All rights reserved
Manufactured in the United States of America

98 97 96 95   4 3 2 1

The paper in this book meets the guidelines for permanence and durability of the Committee on Production Guidelines for Book Longevity of the Council on Library Resources.

Library of Congress Cataloging-in-Publication Data
Walker, Bertrand N. O.
 Tales of the bark lodges / by Bertrand N.O. Walker (Hen-toh) ; with an introduction by Daniel F. Littlefield, Jr., and James W. Parins.
   p.   cm. — (Banner books)
 Originally published: Oklahoma City : Harlow Pub. Co., c1919.
 ISBN 0-87805-794-3 (cloth). — ISBN 0-87805-795-1 (paper)
 1. Wyandot Indians—Folklore. 2. Tales—North America.
 I. Title. II. Series: Banner books (Jackson, Miss.)
E99.H9W35 1995
398.2'0899755—dc20   95-13260
                                       CIP

British Library Cataloging-in-Publication data available

Contents

Introduction vii
Foreword xvii
    I. Old Fox Goes Fishing 3
    II. A Dance and a Dinner 16
    III. Old Coon Sleeps Too Long 27
    IV. Old Fox Meets His Cousin 37
    V. Old Coon Visits the Sugar Bush 51
    VI. Old Fox and Old Coon Both Try a New Venture 61
    VII. A Pre-Historic Race 74
    VIII. The Eagle Feather 84
    IX. Why Autumn Leaves Are Red 95
    X. The Ferryman 100
    XI. Old Coon Teaches the Wolf to Hunt 105
    XII. The Hole in the Sky or How the Summer Became Longer 113

Introduction

Hen-Toh, whose birth name was Bertrand N. O. Walker, was a Wyandot writer of exceptional talent, whose works were never widely circulated and are little known to the reading public today. He was born into the Big Turtle Clan on the Wyandot lands in Kansas on September 5, 1870, the youngest of eight children born to Isaiah and Mary Williams Walker. Isaiah Walker belonged to the Little Turtle Clan of the Ohio Wyandots and Mary to the Big Turtle Clan of the Canadian Wyandots from near Fort Malden. Both descended from Wyandots who figured prominently in tribal history, and both had removed with the Ohio Wyandots to Kansas in 1843. They remained there until 1874, when they removed once more, taking their large family to lands assigned the Wyandots in extreme northeastern Indian Territory.

Hen-Toh's early education aroused a life-long interest in reading and writing. He first attended the federally funded Seneca, Shawnee, and Wyandotte Industrial Boarding School near present-day Wyandotte, Oklahoma. After Hen-Toh left that school, he went briefly to public school at nearby Seneca, Missouri, and then studied for a time with a private tutor. He later took a job as a teacher and began a process of self-education, developing a habit of voracious reading that continued throughout his life.

From 1890 until his death in 1927, Hen-Toh worked in the Indian Service except for brief intervals. He taught for ten years in federal Indian schools in California and Arizona and at the Seneca Industrial School near his home. After 1901 he was a clerk at various Indian agencies but spent most of his time at the Quapaw Agency, which served the Wyandots.

Throughout this period Hen-Toh maintained a home on his allotment, which included the homesite occupied by the Walker family when they removed from Kansas. There he lived during his assignments at the Quapaw Agency, and there he retired when he was between assignments. Even when he was sent to distant agencies, he maintained his home. Surrounded by his large library, historic Wyandot wampum belts, and other family heirlooms, he found an atmosphere conducive to writing and to the study of history and literature. Here, too, he entertained his fellow Wyandots and others, played his piano, and sang.

Hen-Toh demonstrated a bent for writing early in his life. He began his writing career at age eleven when he joined the editorial staff of *The Hallequah*, the monthly school publication of the Seneca, Shawnee, and Wyandotte Industrial Boarding School. Editors were members of the Hallequah Literary Society, which, like other such societies common in federal boarding schools, was organized to foster writing, debate, and oratory among the students. Perhaps part of his literary interests and encouragement grew out of his family's literary background. Peter Dooyentate Clarke was Mary Walker's near relative, their mothers being sisters. The year Hen-Toh was born, Clarke had published his *Origin and Traditional History of the Wyandots*. There was also a well-known literary personage in Isaiah Walker's family. In later years, Hen-Toh kept hanging in his library a picture of his grandfather Walker's famous brother, William Walker: Wyandot chief, diarist, poet, letter writer, orator, politician, and first provisional governor of the Territory of Nebraska.

When Hen-Toh began to write in earnest is uncertain. What is certain is that he aspired first to be a poet. He apparently did not circulate his poems until after 1900, for he was somewhat reticent. He once described himself as "a country boy," saying, "I greatly enjoy meeting people, but do not like to mingle in a crowd." This shyness seems to have carried over into his attempts to get his poems in print. He first sought local outlets such as *Twin Territories* at Muskogee,

Creek Nation, and *Sturm's Statehood Magazine* at Oklahoma City, Oklahoma Territory. Acceptance by these local publications no doubt prompted him to send his work to a national editor in 1906. The editor, however, rejected it as too unusual to be appealing to American readers. Thus rebuffed, Hen-Toh sent his work to *The Indian School Journal,* published at Chilocco Indian School, located in Oklahoma Territory, asking editors to say nothing about him personally and to publish his poems under his Wyandot name. For the next decade, Hen-Toh sent his works, with only two or three exceptions, to the *Journal,* from which they were reprinted in other Indian school and friends-of-the-Indians publications.

In 1918 Hen-Toh left the Indian Service to write full time. During the next four years, he produced works of greater magnitude and of a different quality than most of his earlier works. This shift in Hen-Toh's literary endeavors was apparently the culmination of several forces. Though his earlier works had been primarily poetic, he had published some traditional tales—"Indian Stories Told in the Lodges of the North-east Long Ago" (1907) and "A Wyandotte Myth—Why the Toad Was Called Grandmother" (1911)—which anticipated what would be his best work, the animal stories contained in *Tales of the Bark Lodges.* Hen-Toh may have been spurred to write full time, in part, by an inquiry in early 1918 from the Oklahoma historian Joseph B. Thoburn, who sought answers to some questions about Wyandot culture. Coincidentally, Hen-Toh had been thinking about those same matters and had written an article in 1917 titled "Mon-dah-min and the Redman's Old Uses of Corn as Food," which he had sent to *Country Gentleman*. The magazine's editor had rejected it, Hen-Toh believed, because it was an odd mixture of traditional narrative and discussions of food preparation.

Undaunted by this rejection, Hen-Toh entered a period of intense literary production. In 1919 he published *Tales of the Bark Lodges by Hen-Toh, Wyandot*, which he reprinted the next year in a second edition. Though Hen-Toh returned to Indian Service as clerk at the Quapaw Agency in 1923, he was apparently working on a collection of poems, *Yon-doo-shah-we-ah (Nubbins) by Hen-Toh, Wyandot*, which appeared in 1924. With that volume, his literary career ended. He published little else before his death on June 27, 1927.

In this last, productive period, Hen-Toh worked from models of dialect humor that, though waning in popularity among general readers, had long been popular among Indian writers who were born in the old Indian Territory. Modeling their works after the popular dialect writers in nineteenth-century America, Indian writers of the territory had begun, as early as the 1850s, producing humorous letters, narratives, and anecdotes in the dialects of their individual tribespeople who had learned English as their second language. Near the turn of the century, some had gained widespread popularity, even national notice, such as Alex Posey (Muscogee), whose Fus Fixico letters circulated widely. Hen-Toh was familiar with Posey's work, publicly noting his loss to the literary world when Posey drowned in 1908. His commentary on Posey's Fus Fixico letters indicates his clear understanding of Posey's literary achievement, which Hen-Toh believed would be especially appreciated by readers who were familiar with Indian humor and the dialect in which Posey had couched it. Hen-Toh was also familiar with the work of Royal Roger Eubanks (Cherokee), an artist and writer, who had written and illustrated dialect animal stories similar to Hen-Toh's and published them in 1910.

Hen-Toh chose an Indian persona through which to project not only his narratives but also the poems he published after 1918, for like his contemporary dialect writers and others before them, he believed that with each passing generation, much of traditional culture was lost. He believed that was particularly true of the Wyandots. In earlier days, storytelling was a vital part of Wyandot domestic life, and knowledge was passed orally from generation to generation. Though Wyandot storytelling had declined during his lifetime, Hen-Toh believed he could preserve some of the old stories he had learned as a child through the oral tradition, which persisted during his youth. In later years, Hen-Toh remembered many of the old stories from his childhood and kept them fresh in his mind through his steady contact with tribal members whose lives reached back to far earlier times. His mother, to whom he was very close, had been thirteen at the time of removal and was living as late as 1911. Furthermore, he saw Wyandot elders on a daily basis during his work at the local agency, they visited in his home, and he sought them out. His "Sketches of the Wyandots" (1906) and "Wyandot Research" (1911) had been based on interviews with Wyandots who had made the trek west from Ohio in 1843. Hen-Toh's close contact with old Wyandots had provided him a familiarity with not only Wyandot history and culture but also the rhythms of their English speech. He could have pointed to a number of models for his Wyandot narrative voice.

Tales of the Bark Lodges, then, was Hen-Toh's major effort to preserve some of the traditional tales he had heard. The second edition, which appeared in 1920, was enhanced with illustrations by Eubanks. The son of a well-known translator for the Cherokee Nation, Eubanks was a teacher, writer, artist, and cartoonist.

Without doubt, Hen-Toh chose him as an illustrator because of the interpretive illustrations Eubanks had drawn for his own dialect animal stories a decade earlier. Though attractive, the second edition of Hen-Toh's tales had a small press run and, like the first, did not enjoy wide circulation and quickly went out of print. After seventy-five years, the twelve stories, as they appeared in the 1920 edition, are available to readers once more.

Today's readers will find much that is appealing in the stories. They are full of wit and humor and can be read simply for entertainment. Perceptive readers, however, will recognize the humor, which turns on the games of competition, trickery, and oneupsmanship played among the animals, as a vehicle for valuable lessons in such matters as etiquette, decorum, and mutual respect that formed a base of Wyandot society.

Readers will also find in the stories a demonstration of the art of storytelling. Hen-Toh did not want to preserve the tales by simply retelling them as isolated narratives. He enhanced the charm and flavor of the oral tales by presenting them in dialect, as if told by an old Wyandot woman to a young, part-Wyandot listener in the waning decades of the nineteenth century. The animal stories become, in effect, stories within the story of the Wyandot household to which the boy and his aunt belong. Both become actors in the story. He looks for excuses to have another story told. She, who enjoys telling the stories and needs little prompting, often links the tales by making the action of one grow out of a grudge left over from an earlier episode, especially from the competition between the two central figures, Ol' Coon and his cousin Ol' Fox.

Readers might find parallels between the narrative frameworks for the tales and the frameworks that surround the stories told by Uncle Remus to the little boy in Joel Chandler Harris's stories. In his foreword, Hen-Toh himself notes the parallels between his tales and Harris's, citing the public controversy engaged in by John Wesley Powell of the Bureau of American Ethnology and others concerning whether such stories had their origins in Africa or indigenous America. But like his contemporary Alex Posey and other Indian writers, he defended the Indian origin of the tales.

Despite the perceived parallels, Hen-Toh clearly had in mind some scenes of his early childhood as he shaped the narrative frameworks. The storyteller is modeled after an old aunt who lived in the Walker home, and the little boy, whom she calls "Bra-ty," is Hen-Toh, who was called "Bertie" when he was a child. The father is like Isaiah Walker, who carefully mends the maple-wood bowls that the mother had brought from Canada during the removal. The bowls are reminiscent of those Hen-Toh's mother had brought from her childhood home and had donated in 1911 to the Canadian National Museum in Ottawa.

Through these frameworks, Hen-Toh sets the storytelling scene in winter and makes the storytelling a part of Wyandot domestic life, both of which were proper contexts for storytelling in traditional Wyandot society. Through those contexts and the stories told in them, the reader gains insight into not only the art of storytelling but also the joy of listening.

Daniel F. Littlefield, Jr.
James W. Parins
University of Arkansas, Little Rock

Foreword

More than a quarter of a century ago, among the scattered bands of the Eastern American Indians, were many of the older members of the tribe, whom we among ourselves called, "old time Indians." I refer to those tribes whose ancestors had associated with and known the white man and his ways ever since the earliest Colonial settlements were made.

Amalgamation with the civilized races had lessened the degree of Indian blood and they had become a civilized people. They were educated more or less, and were possessed of an innate refinement of thought and manner. They were reserved, closely observant, earnest and shrewd, and almost always serious. With all that they had gained from civilization, they retained and cherished closely, many of their old manners and customs, adapting these to the ever-changing times. They had a marked character and individuality of their own; and among them were those who, to a discriminating mind, were well worth knowing.

Many of these, however much they had acquired of the ways of others, failed in their use of ordinary English, to the most humorous degree. The greater number of them yet used their own tribal language, and they found it difficult to think something out in this, and then transpose and express it in English. Yet, in spite of the many perplexities, when in the mood to do so, within the family, or circle of intimates, the English language was often spoken to the exclusion of their own. And with all their natural earnestness and seriousness, they would drive straight ahead, paying no attention whatever to the strange and ludicrous quirks and turns they gave to English as they tried to speak it.

They lived much in the past of their race, and they delighted to talk and tell of "the olden times." Lore and legend were very dear to them; and during the long nights of winter, the traditions, tales and myths, handed down from one generation to another for centuries, were often related by these older ones.

I have always loved the old people and their olden tales, and in the broken dialect peculiar alone to the "old time Indian," I have attempted to give some of the old stories originally derived from the Lake Region Tribes. Since these have survived for unknown ages, and have been told and re-told to so many generations; and, since I and many of the friends I have known, have found a certain enjoyment in hearing them related, I have tried to again re-tell some of them for the pleasure of anyone who may find in them anything to please. Perchance, even I, may thereby win another friend.

I have tried also to show somewhat of the individuality and view-point of these old people of the tribe; and it is to the dear memory of those who have long since passed beyond, and to the few that yet remain, that these stories and tales as now given, are dedicated.

Doubtless, there will be some readers, who will at once say that the rights and privileges of "Uncle Remus" have been set at naught. I say: not so; and I believe that my life-long intimate knowledge of Indian life and character entitles me at least to my opinion. Others may have theirs.

I can well recall the time of my boyhood, when I saw the first of the "Uncle Remus Stories." I was delighted with them because I found so much in them with which I had been familiar from my earliest childhood. I hastened to call the attention of the older members of our family to them. And, more particularly did I hasten to read some of them to a dear old Aunt, a Wyandot woman of the old type, who lived with us.

Like myself, she was pleased with them, but at once said as many of the episodes were recognized:

"They're Indian stories; not whiteman; not nigger."

I heartily agreed with her, and while we both

enjoyed them, we were just a bit indignant because, so to speak, our title had been preempted.

Later, when the discussion was taken up by older and far wiser heads than mine, and when Professor Powell of the Smithsonian Institute stated that the stories exhibited more of Indian origin than of negro, I was satisfied as to my claim, and have never since had reason to doubt the fact of their Indian origin.

That the origin of many of the episodes is purely Iroquoian, is to my mind too clear to admit of doubt or dispute. The Cherokee is an Iroquoian tribe, as is also the Wyandot. The Cherokees removed south at an early day in the history of this country and became slave-holders. Can it be doubted that much of their lore, and many of their old tales and traditions were absorbed by the negroes? The Wyandots remained until years later, with their kindred tribes in the north, where these same stories, legends, tales, and traditions had been preserved, with perhaps slight variations among the several tribes, for centuries. Yes, even centuries before such thing was dreamed of, as the coming of either the white man or the black man.

Each of the many stories originally had some special significance which has long since been lost almost entirely. Their preservation was of tribal importance; and it was the duty of some of the older members of the tribe, to relate them to the younger ones. This had been an honored custom among them for untold ages.

Story-telling furnished a vast source of amusement and entertainment, as well as instruction, to the dwellers in the long bark lodges near the Lake shores, during the winter nights. Stories were never related except at this season of the year; for it was the belief that the many spirits of nature thought to be awake and alert during the other seasons, would be perhaps offended at hearing so much said about them. So, in the long, cold, and sometimes dreary winter season, when all nature seemed to be soundly sleeping, time was often whiled away, and even hunger and want forgotten while listening to a story well told.

HEN-TOH, Wyandot.
Ottawa County, Oklahoma.

TALES OF THE BARK LODGES

TALES OF THE BARK LODGES.

I.

OLD FOX GOES FISHING.

"What you sed, Bra-ty? Yooht! You all a time sed tell 'em Ol' Ouendot story. What for? He's 'bout all gone now, Ouendots. You jus' lit'l bit, you fatha', you motha' jus' lit'l bit mo' Ouendot. Look, you hair jus' lik' a sunshine if you ketch 'im an' tie in bunch. Ouendot, his hair black like a night, an' fine, jus' lik you sistah yonda. Eyes black too. He an' you motha' an' me, all looks lik' Ouendot." So spoke a pleasant, kindly looking old Wyandot woman to a little boy who was sitting with her before a cheery open fire, where a row of streaked, juicy red apples were slowly roasting on the broad hearth.

The boy replying to his old aunt, said:

"Yes, I know, but Neh-ah, I'm a Wyandot even if my hair is like what you say, and you know I just love to hear you tell me all of the old stories that the little Wyandot children, yes, and the older ones too, listened to so many, many years ago. That was before they ever knew there was such a thing as a white man, I guess. I like to hear all about the 'olden times' you often tell me about, and how the Wyandots lived and did things then. Anyway, you know that as long as I can claim a little bit of

Wyandot blood, I am an Indian, a Wyandot, and not a white man."

More than just a bit pleased, the old aunt said to him: "Well, I s'pose it's jus' that way, an' it be that way too, all a time, with anybody what's Ouendot. Just say kin' a proud, 'I'm Ouendot.' Anyway, I tole you all a ol' story what I think of, cause you all a time tell a me story 'bout nowadays, an' read to me, book an' pay-pa' too, 'bout eva'thing what's goin' on in worl' an' all a diffunt place. All a Injun long 'go use' tell 'em ol' story, so young folk can le'rn all 'bout ol' times. Some time when hunta's don' got back yet with meat, an' mebbe so don't got much to eat in lodge, then jus' tell 'em story long time, and jus' kin' a fo'got he's hungry. He's do that kin' in a winta' time. But you don' eva' much hungry; anyway look, we have good roas' apple, tzhu-u-wat, prit' soon. Well, anyhow, I tole you 'bout Ol' Fox an' Ol' Coon, at's his couzzen. They jus' all a time try to play trick on each otha' them fellas. Jus' like long time 'go, young fellas what go all 'roun' diffunt village, an' jus' play trick on ol' witch womans, an' eva'body they could, an' jus' make 'em big laff all 'roun' cause they foolish 'em, heap all a time.

"It's col' frosty mornin' long time 'go; winta' time. Ol' Fox he's lazy to get up, jus' sleep long time fo' he get up an' go 'roun' to see what's goin' on. By-um-by, he's jus' walkin' long riva' bank, jus' singin' like to he-self, jus' like he's feelin' kin'-a good. He's jus' come 'roun' by lit'l hill an' he see Coon comin' up road. He's carry somethin' on back, jus' puffin' lik' it's heavy. Ol' Fox he's wonda' what's got Ol' Coon. By-um-by he's come 'long clos', Ol' Coon, an' Fox he see 'em long string, lots crawfish, what's carryin' Ol' Coon.

" 'Good mornin' Couzzen,' he sed it Ol' Coon, 'How you mek it? What fo' you sing jus' like happy, this time mornin'? Mebbe so it's gif you bad lucks, cause you sing so early. Mebbe so you bettah what you say, cut it out.'

"Ol' Fox he jus' grin an' sed: 'Good mornin' Couzzen Coon, I jus' makin' up new song fo' nex' Council Fire; I don' tho't 'bout no bad lucks what you say; but what's you got, all lots a crawfish? Whe-e-e 'at's fine, how you ketch 'em? You jus' all time lucky hunta', ketch eva'thing easy; what makes all a time you do that way?'

"He sed it Ol' Coon: 'Oh, yes, me all time kill 'em ten. 'At's caus' you don't see me come singin' on road befo' I eat 'em my breakfus'; an' this kin', I jus' pick 'em up down riva'. 'At's easy. Seems to me you can do bettah as I can, 'caus' you' tail it's long an' lots a-bushy.'

"Ol' Fox he think he's make a fun 'bout his tail, Coon, an' sed it: 'Oh, it's good 'nuff my tail, but you don' sed how you ketch 'em crawfish; I like to try ketch 'em.'

"'Oh, you lik' ketch 'em,' Ol' Coon, he say, 'It's easy, but you haf to waitin' long time, jus' waitin', but you don't haf to watchin' nothin', jus' waitin'.'

"Fox he say, 'Well, you tell-a-me, an' I do what you sed. I lik' to try to-day, right now.'

"Ol' Coon he point back which way he come an' he say: 'Right down on riva', 'roun' that bank, it's good place on ice, it's lots lit'l hole in ice, all ova'. You look, fin' good one, big nuff jus' put it in, you tail, jus' way down in wata'; he ain't cold much, wata'. You jus' sit there, tail in wata', waitin' long time. By-um-by, crawfish he come 'long l-o-t-s ov 'em, he get all tangle up on you' tail. You jus' waitin' long time; afta' while it's feel heavy, but you jus' waitin' some mo' an' by-um-by when you waitin' l-o-n-g time, you jus' jump quick, jus' high lik' you can. You' tail it's be pull out hole, an' it's all scattah ova' ice crawfish, lots ov 'em. You mus' pick 'em up hurry, fo' he's crawl back to that holes. It's sure bes' kin' fishin I do long time. Sure ketch 'em plenty crawfish, mebbe.'

"Ol' Fox he's jus' lis'n to Coon talk 'bout it, an' he say: 'Well, I try 'im what you sed, Couzzen, cause I lik' to ketch 'em mo' what you ketch 'em, crawfish; I think I go try now.'

"Coon he sed: 'Well, you go try. I'm jus' 'bout froze it now, stan' here tole you 'bout it, fishin'; nobody don' tole me, I jus' mek' 'em that kin' fishin'.' Then he's go on' jus' lik' he's hurry, that Ol' Coon.

He's go lit'l way, an' jus' laff to he-self, much, cause he's jus' foolin' 'im, that Ol' Fox; he don' ketch 'em crawfish that way, lik' what he sed it.

"Fox, he's jus' b'lieve 'im all of it; jus' cause he's got more big tail than Ol' Coon, he's jus' think he ketch 'em heap crawfish. He's go down on ice by riva, jus' hurry, cause he's want fin' hole, so he can do it, that waitin'. He's by-um-by fin' it good one, hole, but it's col' wind blow strong, jus' freezin', but he don' care nothin' cause he's want try that waitin'. He's put in hole his tail, an' he's set down on ice. That ice c-o-l', an' jus' make sheever, jus' lik' eva'thin'. He's jus' think it's be good eatin' that crawfish, an' jus' keep on sheever.

He's don' care fo' that kin', sheever, he's jus' want 'em heaps crawfish.

"By-um-by, it's kin' pull lit'l bit, his tail; it's freezin' that wata', but he don't know, he's jus' think it's much crawfish tangle on his tail. He's think, 'I jus' waitin' some mo' cause it's what mek 'em come lots crawfish. I sure beat 'im, Ol' Coon, ketch'em crawfish, then I tell 'im, I bes' one fishin'.' So that ol' feller, he's jus' waitin', an' waitin' 'til by-um-by, it's his tail all freeze in ice; it's tight one, freeze, you bet'cha.

"He's waitin' lit'l mo', an' sed to he-self: 'It's must-a-be many crawfish now, I think time to jump now.' So he's try to jump high, but it's freeze tight, his tail, an' jus' pull h-a-r-d. He's jus' almos' holler, cause it's make hurt; but he's jus' think it's so lots ov crawfish, he don' care fo' lit'l bit hurt. He's jus' jump h-a-r-d 'notha' time, an' it's almos' pull it off his tail; then he jus' think, 'He's foolish me that Ol' Coon. He tell lie, he don' ketch 'em this way, that crawfish; he's jus' lie all-a-time. He's do me bad one, this trick; but I'll pay back, I ketch 'im. He's fin' out.'

"Well, anyway, it's freeze up his tail, all tight plenty; what's goin' do get 'em loose, don' know, cause it's hurt much eva' time he's try pull 'em. Jus' pull 'em h-a-r-d, it's 'bout break it, his tail. He's feel jus' b-a-d, now.

"By-um-by, he's lookin' 'roun', and' see somethin' lik' black nose, right ova' tha' in hole, clos' to bank; then it's come up lit'l mo' an' it's sharp eye, too, an' Ol' Fox he's sed: 'O Uncle Beaver, I sure got it bad fix, mebbe so you help me.' Ol' Fox he's go 'head tell 'im, Beaver, what's that he's tell 'im do, Ol' Coon. He's tell 'im all 'bout it Ol' Fox. Beaver, he's jus' lis'n, an' look like he's try hard not laff, an' by-um-by he's go back in watah. He's swim ova' unda' ice, an' he's work long time, jus' like eva'thin', and he's get 'em loose Ol' Fox, his tail; then he's come up top 'gen an' tell 'em Ol' Fox: 'Now I guess you pull 'em out ice, you tail, my fren', an' nex' time he's tell you how do somethin', Ol' Coon, mebbe so you don' lis'n good.'

"Ol' Fox he's lis'n what say, Ol' Beaver an' think it; but he's want do somethin',

Old Fox Goes Fishing

too, so he's sed it: 'Uncle, you come, I like fix it somethin' so I 'member it what you do.' Beaver, he jus' come ova' by Ol' Fox, an' Fox he's jus' take hands an' gatha' up lots lit'l sof' white snow, an' he's jus' rub it e-a-s-y all 'roun' it's his nose, Ol' Beaver. It's jus' change color lit'l bit that hairs 'roun' his nose, Ol' Beaver, an' meks look nice, lit'l bit. It's jus' stay that way eva' since.

"That's how he say, Old People, long 'go it's that way."

II.

A DANCE AND A DINNER.

Another evening when the Boy and Neh-ah were sitting before the same cheery fire, while outside the northwest wind swirled and whistled through the bare branches of the walnut trees, Neh-ah, knowing well that a story would soon be asked for, said:

"Bra-ty, I don' tole you 'bout how he's went to Big Council, Ol' Coon, is it? That ol' scamp, he's jus' know he betta' keep out his way, Ol' Fox, lit'l while, anyhow, caus' he's jus' hope Ol' Coon, mebbe so, his couzzen he'll forgot it 'bout that craw-fishin', when he's prit' near los' it his tail.

"Co'se not, he don't fo'get it, Ol' Fox, an' he don' tole nobody 'bout that kin' fishin' neitha'; an' he's jus' hope Uncl' Beaver wouldn' sed 'bout it to nobody too. But that Ol' Beaver, he's good ol' fella, and jus' heap like 'im eva'body; anyhow, he's jus' got tell 'im his fren' that Ol' Otter.

"That Ol' Otter, he's jus' jolly fella, an' all a time jus' laff good 'bout all a kin' a things; an' that Beaver, he's jus' all a time likes to hear 'im laff big, so, jus' tell 'im eva' time, anything, that Otter.

"Any-how—

"It's jus' few days afta' Ol' Coon tole it, his couzzen how to ketch'em crawfish, he sed to he-self, Ol' Coon: 'Mebbe so I get out a way lit'l time, cause Fox he might try it somethin' to get even.' Any how it's jus' 'bout that time, it's come 'Rahshu,' it's what you call 'em moccasin, he's go all 'roun' diffunt village, an' tell 'em somethin', eva'body. He sed this one, it's goin' be big Council way down 'notha place.

"Ol' Coon he's always like to go, cause he's good singa', an' he's talk good sometimes, too. Anyhow he sed: 'I go, bet'cha Ol' Fox he's don' be there.' Then he's jus' laff, an' he sed: 'I tell 'em all those fellas how's Ol' Fox he's ketch'em crawfish.'

"So's he's get ready an' he's go. He's fin' lots of 'em that place when he's got there. Somebody he sed: 'Where is it Ol' Fox an' Turtle, it's always come them fellas, wonda' where is it an' why don' come.' But afta' while Ol' Coon tell 'em 'bout how ketch'em crawfish, Ol' Fox, he don' say that no mo', jus' laff good.

"They all stay that place three-fouh days, talkin' 'bout lots thing, then Coon, he sed: 'Well, time I go,' an' he's pick up his lit'l drum an' start back. He's jus' travel 'long all day, sometime he's sing lit'l bit, sometimes he's talk to he-self. He neva' see nobody, 'til he's jus' 'bout home, when sun, he's 'bout go ova' hill; then he's meet Turtle, jus' comin' 'long slow, he's goin' home too.

" ' 'Kway, my fren'!' he's sed it, Ol' Coon, 'What fo' you don' bin there, Big Council? We look fo' you, all time, we want you make good talk.'

"Ol' Turtle, he sed: 'I goin' bin there, but jus' when I start, Ol' Fox, his woman he come my lodge, an' he sed somethin' wrong Ol' Fox, he's bad cross, don' like nothin'. He want me come see 'im, Ol' Fox. So I tell 'im I go see Ol' Fox, mebbe so he's sick, I doctah him. So, I go see him, but I can't know what's mattah with 'im. He's jus' cross like dickens all time, an' it's heap sore, his tail.'

"Ol' Coon he's jus' lis'n an' laff lit'l bit, then he sed: 'Ol' Fox, he be a'right in few day. I go, now, I gotta' fin' suppa' some kin'.' So he's go on. By-um-by he's come out of bush, right by lake, oh it's nice one, that lake, jus' blue watah and jus' clos' to sho' it's swim 'roun' lots of goose;

he's fat one, too. Ol' Coon, he's jus' look at those lots of goose, then he say: 'Yo-ho, my fren's, you come, I tell it you somethin'; where I jus' come, it's eva'body jus' sing an' dance. It's new dance. You fellas jus' come out on nice sand, I show you how do it.' It's all those goose, he jus' come step out on sand, jus' walk like soldier, long string. Ol' Coon jus' take off belt, his lit'l drum, an' sed it: 'Well, my fren's, you jus' make it big ring, I stay in middel. I sing an' beat it drum. When I stop sing an' play drum, all you gooses jus' shut eyes tight an' dance slow jus' like what I showed you now.' Then Ol' Coon he's jus' dance nice to show 'em how, all those goose. He say, Ol' Coon: 'You musn't stop dance 'till I begin sing 'gen, an' jus' keep shut all time, yo' eye. It's how they dance eva'body, down that place I jus' come now.'

"So all that gooses jus' make ring, like he's tol' 'em Ol' Coon, an' all jus' shut his eye an' list'n while he's sing good, Ol' Coon, an' jus' beat it that drum. He's jus' sing:

> 'Ho-he-yah, ho-ha,
>   Yah-dra-wah, ho-ye-yah,
> Ho-ha, yah-dra-wah.'

"Then when Ol' Coon, he quit singin', all those old goose jus' dance 'roun' slow an' easy like, all his eye jus' shut. Now Ol' Coon jus' reach out queek, an' grab one ol' fat she-goose, jus' snap his head off 'fore he could squawk, an' thro'

it behin' him in hurry. Then he's sing agen, an' when he's stop sing, those goose jus' dance 'roun' slow like, an' he grab 'notha one, fat one, an' queek, twis' head off an' throw behin' him, then he do same thing, an' get notha' one. But jus' when he's ketch 'em las' one, lit'l ol' she-goose dancin', open one eye jus' lit'l bit, cause he want see if he ain't bes' dancer. That she-goose when he see what he's do that Ol' Coon, jus' holler loud an' sed: 'Oh, he's kill us!' an' all those goose he's fly 'way, like big hurry.

"Ol' Coon he's jus' laff, an' pick 'em up his three goose an' lit'l drum, an' start on to his lodge. He's think he's got good suppa' now.

"While he's goin' 'long, he's say to heself: 'I b'lieve I like 'em betta' roas' gooses.' So when he's come his lodge, he's fix his gooses, an' pick up lots of stick to mek big fire, cause by-um-by it's burn all down an' meks good lots coal an' ashes, good place to roas' 'em gooses. It's good suppa' he's got now, by-um-by, soon.

"It's w-a-y down 'long river, Ol' Fox, his lodge. By-um-by he's look out an' see big light, big fire on hill clos' by his lodge, Ol' Coon. Ol' Fox he look, an' he say to heself: 'I wonda' he's come home, that ol' rascal, an' what fo' he's got big fire. I jus' slip 'roun' that way an' see what he's do.' So he's call his little nephew what's live with him, an' tole 'im don't need to mek fire in lodge, cause he's goin' 'way an' not come back 'til late. It's what he sed, Ol' Fox, an' tell 'em nephew: 'You go sleep.'

"Well, 'bout that time, his fire, Ol' Coon, it's all burn down, an' make good ashes an' hot coal. He's take stick an' scrape all 'way that hot coal, an' lay 'em down that gooses on his back, all, one, two, three, in row, his foot all stick up straight out ashes jus' like beans what's jus' come up in garden.

"It's gettin' dark now, an' wind it's blow. He could hear 'im up in limbs on tree. Ol' Coon, up high on rocky hill, he's set down by fire an' jus' lis'n. He's kin' tired that Ol' Coon, an' it's jus' soun' easy that wind, an' make 'im feel sleepy like. He's lis'n to riva' down there, too, jus' soun's good, an' by-um-by he's jus' sleepy like eva'thing. So, he say to he-self: 'I could take it nap while it's cook, my suppa', I do that 'cause nothin' botha it 'tall.'

"It's some limbs way up high ova he head, jus' makin' noise 'cause wind it's blow and jus' mek squeek when it's rub togetha' that limbs. Ol' Cool he's sed: 'Hey, you noisy fellas up tha', I want sleep lit'l nap, you woke me if it's botha anythin' 'bout my suppa'. He's say a'right that limbs, an' by-um-by that Ol' Coon he's curl up an' sleep good, jus' lit'l ways from fire."

III.

OLD COON SLEEPS TOO LONG.

A stick of wood in the fire-place burned in two, and the sparks went flying up the chimney's black throat. The Boy took the poker and drew the other logs closer together. Meanwhile the tall old clock struck off eight resounding peals, finishing with its usual whirr.

"Neh-ah, it only said eight, can't you go on and tell me if that poor Old Coon, hungry as he was, got to eat his fine supper; or did it all burn up while he was taking such a good nap. He made such a great fire, I'm wondering."

After turning to the boy's mother, who was sitting near by sewing, and addressing a few words to her in Wyandot, the Old Aunt said:

"No, it don' burn it up, his suppa'. Spec' he don' bin so mad if it did. He no bizness lay there an' go sleep it so good; but he's jus' all a time such a smart, it's jus' good 'nough fo' him. I tole you lit'l mo' 'bout it, then you go bed.

"Well,

"It's a'ready come up, big moon, down tha' in east; but it's jus' sleepin' yet, Ol' Coon, don' wake 'im up, nothin'. By-um-by, up there in rocks, 'bove where it's sleepin,' Ol' Coon, you could see 'em sharp nose an' sharp eyes too, jus' 'roun' edge of rock, lookin' down where's sleep, Ol' Coon. Then when see he's sleep good, that Coon, Ol' Fox he's come down, jus' walkin' easy, he don't step on rocks, no nothin', jus' walk sof' an' don' mek it noise. He's look all 'roun' that Fox, an' by-um-by he's see 'em that six goose foots stickin' out row in ashes.

"'Ah-e-e-e,' he jus' sed it easy, 'that's reason he's got big fire, Ol' Coon. I glad I'm fin' it, an' I glad I'm come see 'bout it that big fire. I lik' 'em roas' gooses, an' I could jus' 'bout eat 'em three of it. He's good one, hunta, my Couzzen; but must a-be it's heap tired now. Too tired, can't eat 'em; well, I eat 'em that goose.'

"He's look at that Ol' Coon all-a-time, but he's jus' sleepin' good now, so Fox he's jus' step 'roun' easy an' get stick, an' scrape 'way ashes from that gooses. It's roas' nice, an' jus' smell good. It's some limbs up there in trees jus' sque-e-k, but it don' botha' him, Ol' Coon.

"Fox, he's get busy eat it that goose an' by-um-by it's jus' nothin' lef' but pile bones—it's got lots meat on yet, cause he's jus' eat it bes' part, that Fox. He's got nuff fo' he's eat all of it; jus' can't eat no mo'. It's jus' sque-e-k all-a-time that limbs, but don' wake it up nothin' that Ol' Coon.

"When he's eat all he want, that Fox, he pick up all-a bones an' put 'em back in ashes, an' he's cova' all up 'gen jus' lik' it's don' botha' it nothin'; an' he's

stick in row 'gen, all that goose foots in ashes, jus' same lik' he's fix it, Ol' Coon.

"It's lit'l pile sof' ashes clos' by, an' he's go there, Ol' Fox, an' he's jus' dance all ova' it, so's he could fin' it his tracks, that Ol' Coon when he's wake up. He sed it: 'I think my couzzen he bin glad I come see 'im, he bin glad I don' woke 'im up, cause he's heap tired.'

"He's jus' fix it eva'thin' that Fox, then he's go down hill towa'ds riva'. It's fine night, moonlight, an' he's jus' walk 'long riva' bank 'til he's feel kinda' tired and sleepy-like—that's cause he's eat so much goose. By-um-by he's come to big one tree what's stan' 'way out ova' riva'. It's look like good place to sleep, so he's clim' up an' fin' good place to stretch out, an' by-um-by he's go sleep. Big moon, it's yellow, shine jus' ova' that Fox, down through limbs what don' got no leaf on it, and mek good shadow that Fox down in clear wata; it's jus' lik' he's down tha' in wata, that Fox.

"Well, by-um-by up on hill, that Ol' Coon he's jus' wake up in hurry an' he's sed: 'I guess I take good nap, mebbe.' An' he's jus' stretch he-self an' look 'roun'. He's jus' think: 'Well, I got good suppa' anyhow, must-a-be cook good now.'

"He's go in hurry ova' to fire an' reach out bofe hands an' ketch holt goose foots to lif' it out of ashes. He's jus' lif' kind-a hard, lik' it's heavy, an' he's jus' tumble back an' roll ova' holdin' that goose foots in his hand. He's jus' feel lik' funny, an' he say: 'I guess it's cook too much, my suppa'."

"He's get up an' go ova' there fire 'gen, an' take it out that otha' goose-foots one at time. He's don' know what's mattah, an' he's jus' look lik' funny' eva' time he's take it out that goose-foots; then he's take stick an' scrape 'way that ashes, an' don' fin' nothin' jus' pile bones with lit'l bit meat on it. He's jus' much mad, an' he's sed it:

" 'He's jus' bin here, some lazy thief an' steal it my supper. I jus' like to seen it, I bet I bust 'im his nose. I jus' like to fin' out who done it, I bet I poun' it good. Must-a-be it's that Ol' Fox, he's the one. He's jus' think he's get even fo' that crawfishin' I tol' 'im how to do it. 'At jus' joke, that one. It's m-e-a-n trick, this one. It's a' right for him, jus' wait I ketch 'im, I poun' 'im an' lick 'im good, I don' care fo' hund'ed snakes, how much he's holler, when I fin' 'im.' He's jus' get madda' all time that Ol' Coon, an' he's jus' shake his fist at those limb up in trees, an' sed: 'What fo' you don' do it like I sed it, wake me up when I sleep it? I tole you that way, ain't it?' He's jus' pickin' meat off those bone, while he's scold it that limbs, an' he's jus mad like eva'thing. He's jus' scold som' mo' that limb, and sed it:

" 'What fo' you don' keep still now, you don' have to mek noise, you jus' mek me mad all a time. If don' stop you mekin' noise, I come up tha' when I finish pick this bones, an' I mek you stop.' That limb he's jus' keep on squeek, sqe-e-e-k, all-a-time, an' it's so mad that Ol' Coon jus' hurry and' eat that bones, so he could go up an' whip it those limb.

"When he's get thro' eatin' that bone, he jus' look 'roun' and' by-um-by he's fin' it that place where he's dance, Ol' Fox. Ol' Coon he's fin' it that tracks, an' when he's look at it, he's jus' m-a-d, some mo'. An' he's jus' pick on that limbs som' mo', an' sed it: 'I jus' come up tha' an' I fix it you fellas.' So he's jus' go up that trees 'til he's come to that place where that limb it's kin' a broke, an' it's in fork, an' wind it's blow an' jus' make it that noise where it's rub. Ol' Coon, he's jus' take hold that big limb with bofe han's an' he's jus' goin' throw down. He's so mad he don' see that mebbe so might pinch 'im that limbs, cause it's jus' swing. Fust he's know it' just ketch 'im his hand, that limb, an' just pinch 'im tight. Oh, it's hurt like eva'thing. He's jus' pull an' pull, that Coon, an' jus' make worse. By-um-by he's pull it out; but it's hurt b-a-d his hand. He's sure get hard time, that Ol' Coon. He's jus' slip off try to sleep mebbe."

IV.

OLD FOX MEETS HIS COUSIN.

It had been snowing, and outside a keen, sharp north wind was rioting everywhere. The Boy, having finished his evening chores, came in with some hickory logs for the fire-place.

The fire-light alone lit up the room, and the old brass andirons glinted in its glow. Neh-ah was sitting in her usual place, and the Boy, taking his, said:

"Neh-ah, this is a fine evening for some more stories about Old Fox and Old Coon. I know it is so cold outside that no snakes or grass-hoppers or anything else will hear you telling them."

"Yooht! What fo' you don' get tired hear 'em ol' story? Jus' seem like you want it all a time, ol' story. Guess you betta' go you' Uncl' Jim, Canada, cause he could tole you that kin' Injun story, all kin' 'til you get tired to lis'n. Long 'go when we all young folks, we go down Gram'ma Hunt, his house, winta' time, an' jus' lis'n to ol' story, lots of 'em. Was bes' one to tell 'em story, Gram'ma Hunt. Neva' did get tired to lis'n, an' he's jus' lik' it to tole us that kin' too. Only was some kin' story jus' fo' ol' folks, he don' tole to us that ones.

"What 'bout I tole you las' time? Oh, yes, Ol' Coon he's los' it his good gooses suppa', an' Ol Fox he's bin fill up plenty.

"Well, seems like when Ol Coon so mad an' mek that big talk 'bout how he's lick 'im that Fox, he's heard 'im sed it, that Mista' Skunk; so that Skunk, he's jus' go right now an' tole 'im 'bout it that Fox what he's sed it that Coon, how he's goin' lick 'im. Then he mad, that Fox, and he tell 'im Skunk: 'You jus' see, I lick that Coon, myself, fust time I seen it.'

"He' don' had no chance fo' few day tho', cause that Coon he's jus' stay at home, cause it's bad sore, his hand.

"One night, it's kin'a late, that Coon he's think, 'I guess I go ketch 'em crawfish.' So he's go down by riva' an' ketch 'em good many, take 'em his lodge an' have good suppa'. He don' take it no naps this time.

"When he's done his suppa' he's jus' think, 'I take lit'l walk cause don' bin no where, long time.' So he's start out 'long riva bank. Eva'thing jus' seem like good to that Ol Coon, he's jus' trot 'long sing low like to he-self. He's jus' like happy, an' jus' keep on goin'. By-um-by he's get sleep like, an' jus' wish he's back his lodge; but it's long ways, so he sed it: 'I fin' some place take nap.' Right that time he's come 'long clos' by that big tree what he's seen it Ol' Fox. Jus' grow leanin' ova' wata.' Ol' Coon, he's think it good place, so he's clim' up in lit'l fork

OLD FOX MEETS HIS COUSIN.

limb. He's jus' fix good 'bout go sleep, an' he's hear somethin'.

"It's big moon yet, an' jus' bright. Ol' Coon he's look down riva'-bank an' he's see it comin' Ol Fox, jus' trot 'long trail. He's jus' keep still, Ol' Coon, like he's sleep; but he's look straight down unda' him an' he's see his shadow in wata', looks jus' like him. He's look at that Ol' Fox an' he's lookin' at that shadow, too. He's jus' lookin' m-a-d, an' Ol' Coon he's hear him sed it, Ol' Fox: 'Here it is that Coon, in wata' lookin' fo' craw-fish now. I jus' slip up an' jump on 'im give 'im lickin'.' So, Fox he's jus' slip up edge riva'-bank, eye jus' snappin'. He jus' mek big jump down in wata' where he think it that Coon. He jus' make it b-i-g splosh, an' prit' soon come up top wata' an' he's jus' sputtah an' blow b-i-g, jus' like almos' choke 'im. Then he's hear that Coon up in tree jus' laff l-o-u-d, an' say: 'Hey, Couzzen, it's early to swim, ain't it? I hear Gran'fatha Turtle he sed it, you mustn't jump when you don' look, an' you mustn't be too hurry.'

"That Fox he's crawl out on bank an' he's jus' sheever. He don' sed nothin', jus' commence pick up stick an' brushes an' pile it foot of tree, lit'l ways clos' to mek fire. He's put l-o-t-s stick an' mek it big fire, an' when it's burn good, he's jus' sit down foot that tree, that Fox, jus' like he stay there' till he's come down tree, that Coon.

"Prit' soon, Coon he's sed it: 'My Couzzen, sure you not goin' set tha' long time. You coat lots wet, mebbe so ketch 'em bad cold. I glad to come down talk to you, mebbe so gif some my tobacco to smoke, cause must-a-be wet yours afta' you jump in riva'. I spec' I stay here tho', it' best one, cause I could see good up this tree. Mebbe so somebody comin' long to botha' you, I seen it an' tole you 'bout it.'

"Ol Fox he don' sed nothin', jus' set by fire, back up 'gainst tree, an' jus' keep it shut, his mouth. It's hard work tho', that kin'. That Coon he could drop in wata' an' get 'way; but he jus' think he's stay in tree an' talk an' foolish 'im his couzzen.

By-um-by, he sed it: 'Well, I sleep it lit'l bit now.' So, he's curl up an' sleep it.

"Afta' long time he's woke up. It's shine bright, big moon, 'way high. He's look down an' its settin' by tree yet, that Fox, jus' soun' sleep it. Coon' he's jus' slip down e-a-s-y, 'til he's clos' to that Fox. He sleep it good, could heard 'im snore. Coon, he's jump easy down on groun'. He don' move nothin' that Fox, sure 'nough sleep it. He's bad one, that Ol' Coon, he's jus' take it long one, stick, dry leaf on end, an' he's tickle it his nose, that Fox; but he's so sleep don' botha' him nothin'.

"That bad one, Ol' Coon, he sed it to heself: 'It prit' good chance, mebbe so I make it 'notha' tricks on my couzzen.'

"So, he's jus' slip 'long down by riva'-bank where he fin' it lots sticky mud, it's red. He's get big one, chunk, that muds an' jus' spread on flat rock, an' put it on wata', jus' stir lit'l bit an' make it heap sticky, just like what you call it, moh-lass. Then he's took it that muds an' jus' rub all ova' his face, that Fox, put lots that muds on his eye. He's jus' step back lit'l bit, that Coon, an' look at him, that Fox, an' he's jus' laff good to he-self, an' sed it: 'My poor couzzen sure have good time to wash it face in mornin', if it's dry good that muds. I spec' I start home now, mebbe so it's time.'

"Well, he's started that Ol Coon an' go lit'l piece, then he's jus' roll ova' on groun' an' jus' laff big at that Fox 'till he's tired.

"It's 'bout gone that moon, jus' comin' daylight in east, when he's woke up that Fox. What's matta'? He's woked up sure; but can't see nothin', can't open it his eye, not jus' lit'l bit. He's jus' stagger an' run into stump an' bush, jus' fall down, almos' tumble in riva'. It be good thing he did, cause soak it up that muds; but he don' done it.

"He's jus' rub it that dried muds but he don' come off, an' eye jus' stick 'em tight shut, can't open. He's sure bad fix this time, an' jus' m-a-d like dickens. Jus' sed it all a bad name could think of 'bout that Ol' Coon, jus' cuss him heap, I guess. It's don' do no good that kin' tho'.

OLD FOX MEETS HIS COUSIN.

"Well, he try to find path go to his lodge, but jus' get tangle up in briar-patch, an' it's stuck 'im all ova'. It's b-a-d lucks fo' him that Fox, sure. He jus' don' know what do nex'. So, he's jus' set still lit'l bit, study what do. Prit' soon he's hear, tap, tap, tap, on dead limb 'way up high his head. He's lis'n 'gen an' heard it, tap, tap, tap.

" 'Yoh-ho, my fren',' he's sed it, 'come here, got big trouble me, mebbe so you could he'p it.'

"It's come fly down hurry, that lit'l speckle wood-pecker bird, an' sed it; 'What's mattah, my fren', what I can do he'p it you now?'

"Fox he say: 'I like to have you tried

it, pickin' this dry muds off my eye, so's I could see how open it my eye.'

"'Mebbe so, it's too much sharp my bill', it's sed it that wood-pecker bird. 'I pick 'em prit' hard, but I see what I do, I don' hurt you, I can he'p it.' So it's go to work, wood-pecker bird, jus' set on end his nose, that Fox, an' pick 'em e-e-a-s-y as can, but it's sure make 'im come blood, cause it's sh-a-r-p that wood-pecker bird, his bill. Well, that Fox he could see how open it his eye, prit' soon an' jus' looks good to him, eva'thing. That lit'l bird tell 'im to washin' his face good in riva'.

"That Ol' Fox, he's feelin' kin' a good 'gen, an' jus' thank it that wood-pecker bird, an' sed it: 'What I can do fo' you, my fren', cause you sure do big he'p with me?'

"That lit'l wood-pecker bird he sed it: 'Oh, my fren', long time I jus' wish I could had it on my head, lit'l spot, red jus' l-e-e-t'l one spot, not big one like he's got, Great Wood-pecker, Quank-quank-queh.'

"Fox he's sed it: 'That's good, my fren', I fix it that lit'l spot, red one.' So he's took it some blood on his face where it's drop down, an' he's paint it lit'l spot, red one, on his head, that lit'l she wood-pecker bird. It's jus' stay there, too, that spot, eva' since.

"Oh, he's so glad that lit'l she wood-pecker bird, jus' fly up in tree an' try his bes' sing, but can't do it much. Well, he's got it red spot anyway, an' jus' lots happy.

"That Fox, he's jus' trot off on trail 'long riva' an' try to think what could do get even with him, that Coon."

V.

OLD COON VISITS THE SUGAR BUSH.

The Father had been mending a crack in one of the Mother's treasured old maple-wood bowls, made more than a century ago by a Wyandot, when the tribe lived in Canada, along the beautiful Detroit.

The Boy having watched the work of pouring the melted lead into the broken place in the bowl, turned to his aunt and said:

"Neh-ah, you and I will make sugar this year. We'll tap the trees down along the bluff, and have some real maple syrup. We can take our lunch every day and have a sure enough camp. You can tell me stories while we boil down the sap."

Neh-ah nodded assent and replied:

"Yes, that jus' like you, always think some way to get story. Anyhow, I don' tole you yet, what he's do nex' Ol' Fox an' Coon, an' what you talk 'bout 'minds me of it. He's always mek it maple-suga' Ouendots. It's lots a work, too, but he don' care fo' that. Could jus' keep 'im busy do somethin' all a time. Don' had no clock, no ah-man-ac them days, tell 'em how much time gone. I spec' don' get ol' so quick, peoples them days."

"Well, days bin get lit'l long, sun he's start go back north. It's time come bright night an' frosty mornin', an' kin' a warm sunshine day-time. It's jus' 'bout time go suga'-bush, those people, tap tree an' mek 'em maple suga'. Jus' make lots of it, put in mo-cocks, use in winta' time. It's kin' a hard works mek'em suga' them days, 'cause got to mek-em lots trough birch-bark, ketch'em sap. He's got b-i-g trough too, mek'em out a big log. Don' had no kettle them days; jus' have to put 'em hot rock in big trough; but he don' care fo' nothin' them peoples, don' care fo' hundred snakes, 'cause he's jus' got lots a times, them days. Don' got no times do nothin' now days.

"Jus' 'bout this time year, he's jus' like it to follow them peoples to suga-bush, that Coon. He's alway jus' like it, poke 'roun' in suga'-camp, come night, an he's sleep it them peoples. That Ol' Coon he's jus' l-i-k-e it to put it his nose in trough an' drink it lit'l bit sap, s-w-e-e-t one. He like it good that sap, an' sometime if he don' found it in lit'l trough, he's try to get one drink out'a that b-i-g trough. It's hard to do that one tho', cause mebbe it's prit' hot that sap in big trough, an' it's always jus' keep cover up that big trough with nice boa'ds, white ones, jus' mek it out'a lin-wood, them peoples.

"Afta' he's put it on that Fox that dry muds, it's long time no seen each otha' that Fox an' that Coon. He jus' thought it Ol' Coon, it's prit' near even to him, that Fox; an' mebbe so he won't try nothin' notha' kin' tricks. He don' want see 'im tho', an' jus' keep out a way, cause he might try mek' 'notha' tricks on 'im, that Fox. It's jus' go on that way fo' days, an' Ol Coon jus' 'bout think: 'Well, I guess mebbe so he's fo'get it, that las' trick, my couzzen.'

"But that Fox, he don' fo'get it nothin', no seh. He's prit' sharp, an' he jus' all a time got it, that what you call 'em— 'watch-full-a-waitin'. He's know it Ol Fox, 'bout his couzzen all a time likes to foolish 'roun' that suga'-bush, when that peoples he's mekin' suga', an' he's know it how he like it to drink that sap, heap s-w-e-e-t. So, he's just keep it, his 'watch-full-a-waitin,' an' when Skunk tole 'im: 'Ole Coon not home, bin gone three-fou' days,' that Fox jus' sed it: 'I spec' mebbe so it's gone suga'bush, my couzzen, I guess I go see.'

"Well, he's start that Fox to go suga'-bush. It's fine days an' when gets there, jus' see all a peoples heap busy, work. Fox he's jus' slip 'roun' edge ov camp, all-a-time he's lookin' fo' sign ov that Coon. He's look l-o-n-g time, an' by-um-by he's fin' tracks 'long edge lit'l branch, that Coon' he's bin lookin' crawfishes, mebbe so.

"It's late in evenin', while he's sleep it some place that Coon, Ol' Fox he's jus' get busy. Afta' that peoples he's gone to all lit'l ones, trough, to get it, sap, Fox he's come 'long behin', an' he's jus' turn it, bottom up, eva' one that lit'l trough. Then he's go look in big trough. It's prit' near full sap, it's hot.

"So he's sne-e-k 'roun' some mo' an' watch it good ol' squaw cover it big trough, all good with that white boa'd. He's jus' watch it 'roun' 'till it's all fix it, eva'thing, an' them peoples it's all sleep it. Then that Fox he's slip up by big trough, an jus' push it two that boa'ds, lit'l 'ways' part.

"Well, he's jus' push it ova' them two boa'ds 'til end of it right on edges ov big trough. It's smell good that sap, prit' near mak' 'em Fox want some he-self; but he don' botha' it, 'fraid might ketch 'im his own trap, I spec'. When he's all done fix it, that Fox, he's jus' go lit'l ways, hide in bushes an' watch for him, that Coon. He's wait long time, an' by-um-by he's hear it comin' somebody, jus' grumblin' to he-self. It's that Ol' Coon, an' Fox he's hear him sed it: 'Wonda' what fo' so steengy, them peoples; jus' turn 'em upside bottom all lit'l trough. Can't fin' lit'l bit sap. Mebbe I could get drink on big trough if don' turn it upside bottom, too.'

"Ol Fox he's keep it still, jus' kin' a chuckle tho', cause he knows goin' ketch 'im that trap what he fix it fo' Ol' Coon.

"That Coon jus' come pokin' long slow like, till he fin' it that big trough. He's jus' walk all 'roun' kin' a easy, jus' sniffin' an' lookin' fo' crack. Fox he's fix it chunk right front where he's fix it that boa'ds, an' that Ol Coon he's jump on that chunk,

his nose stick up in air, an' jus' get good whiff that saps. It's kin' a hot. Well, he's set on chunk lit'l bit an' jus' lookin roun'. He don't seen nothin', then he's jus' mek 'notha' jump an' he's lan' right on end ov that boa'ds what's he push it ova' that Fox. That boa'ds he jus' slide ova' otha' way queek, an' that Ol Coon he's jus' go ker-plum in that hot saps.

"Them boa'ds make big rattle noise an' it's wake 'im up that Ol' Squaw. He's come out lodge see what's matta' an' come by that big trough jus' time he's crawl out Ol' Coon. He's got big stick in his han' that squaw, an' jus' hit that Coon good whack on side when he's run 'way. He's jus' go hurry, Ol' Coon, an' by-um-by when he's go thro' bush, somebody sed it: 'Hoh, Couzzen, you like it to take good wash in hot sap, ain't it? Mebbe so ain't good 'nough wata'?"

VI.

OLD FOX AND OLD COON BOTH TRY A NEW VENTURE.

"Neh-ah, you said there was one more story about Old Fox and Old Coon and that it was a long one, too. Now, this evening while everyone else is gone and just you and I are sitting by the fire, won't you tell it to me? I'll go down cellar and get some of those apples we like so well, and we'll have a regular party."

After his return with the apples, and after putting some hickory logs on the fire, the Boy seated himself in his accustomed place and waited for the story.

"I wonda' what's goin' do when it's all gone, story. If you bin live long time 'go, ol' man they took you, an' jus' mek story tella' out o' you, so you could tell 'em all a young mans when you get be ol' man. Nowdays jus' have book an' noose-paypa' an' eva'thing an' write down. It's seem funny to Injun first time he know that kin', jus' think white man mek paypa' talk. Mebbe so you could write it somethin' story, some day, then won't have tell 'em, just could read it' anybody.

"Las' time, that Ol' Coon jus' bin foolin' 'roun' suga'-camp, aint it? Good fo' nothin' jus' spoil it all big trough sap fo' that poor ol' Injun woman. Anyhow, 'bout that time, spring jus' begin think 'bout turnin' ova'.

"Them days jus' get some mo' long. South wind, he's come now an' mek it all broke up ice in riva' an' jus' go float 'way. It's kind a blue smoky all 'roun' an' you could smell it that brush an' leaf it's bin burnin', caus' it's garden patch clean up them peoples. Buds on tree it's swell up an' no mo' peoples in suga'bush, all gone back to village. Prit' soon plant corn patch, when leaf on hick'ry tree 'bout big as squirrel, his ear.

"That Coon don' see it, Ol' Fox, since time Ol' Coon he's fall in big trough. Somebody sed it he's gone mek visit with fren' 'way down end of lake, Ol' Fox.

"Coon, he's jus' study all a time how get even on that Fox fo' las' trick he's bin play. Jus' think all kinds, cause he's want make 'em bes' trick yet on that Fox, cause he's prit' mad to him yet.

"Well, South Wind he's drive it all 'way that snow and ices, even that patches 'long north side hills. Early mornin' you could heard it lots wild gooses and duck. Jus' go, 'honk, honk,' like what you call it—auto'bile, when jus' go 'long road like dickens, an' seen somethin, in road, nowdays. That goose an' ducks he's comin' back from south, an' he's jus' stop ova', visit few days all 'long. Could fin' it lots good eat in marsh 'long riva', jus' 'fore it's run in lake.

"Ol' Coon an' eva-body jus' glad to see come back, an' jus' holla to him somethin' when he's fly ova. He's all a time glad ketch 'em two-three, too, if he could do it, foolish 'em or somehow.

"One day, sun mo' than half ova', Ol' Coon he's start out try to ketch 'em goose. It's lots of 'em down marsh, an' he's want try new way ketch 'em. He's jus' slippin' 'long e-a-s-y like, riva'-bank, an' he's meet 'im Lit'l Fox, it's his nephew, Ol' Fox. He's live with 'im, his uncle, an' he's treat 'im mean, all a time, that uncle. Jus' mek 'im work hard, that po' lit'l nephew, an' feed 'im nothin' 'cep' scraps. Eva-body know that kind, an' jus' feel sorrow fo' it, cause that uncle jus' whip it an' mean to it all a time. He's prit' near starve', you could count it his rib, an' jus' few hair on it, his tail. Seem like, all a time, he's goin' dodge somethin' that lit'l fella'.

"His garden-patch, Ol' Fox, it's good one, beans, pumpkin, eva'thing all good; cause that nephew an' his aunt jus' work it plenty. Ol' Fox, he don't work lit'l bit, but he's jus' all a time brag it that garden-patch, an' he's always tole it that nephew: 'Took care of it my garden-patches.'

"Well, that time when he's met 'im Ol' Coon, that Lit'l Fox, he's look like he feel prit' good, that lit'l fella, an' he's tole it to Ol' Coon, his uncle bin gone on visit 'way down lake. Ol Coon he's always feel sorrow for 'im, that lit'l fella,' an' jus' all a time be good to him. Jus' take him go hunt, an' showed it an' tole it lots a things

THEY TRY A NEW VENTURE.   67

'bout how to hunt. He's tole 'im tho' musn't tell 'im you uncle, cause it jus' mek 'im mean to lit'l fella' some mo'. So, when he seen 'im that time, Ol' Coon, he's sed it: 'Well, Lit'l Fella', my couzzen, what you look fo' this time, is it come home you uncle?'

"Lit'l Fox he's say: 'Mebbe so he's come back tomorro' mornin'. Mr. Skunk he's tole him las' night, my aunt, when he's stop lit'l bit our lodge. We bin all clean up garden-patches, an' I jus' think I go hunt it some game.' Ol' Coon sed it: 'Well, young fella', jus' stayed by me. I got good way, new one, try to ketch 'em gooses, mek 'em good one dinner, bofe of us, mebbe.' Lit'l fella, he sed it: 'Uncle, you all a time mek good one, hunt, good one ketch 'em, all a time kill 'em ten, I spec' so we ketch 'em heap this time.'

"So, they jus' trot 'long togetha' an' Ol' Coon jus' 'splain 'bout that new way ketch 'em gooses. He's goin' fin' it lit'l bunch gooses what's bin eat plenty, an' jus' swimmin' 'roun', prit' clos' to sho.' Cause if he belly full, he don' think 'bout nothin' botha' 'im, he's sed it, that Coon. He's got long rope, lit'l one, what he's made out sof' bark. It's stout one, too, an' he's tie on it that rope, three-fou' slip-knot. When he's fin' it lit'l bunch gooses, he's goin' dive in wata' an' swim unda' where's that gooses, an' put it that slip-knots ova' his foots, many as he wants them gooses. Jus' jerk 'em queek an' swim to bank an' pull 'em in them goose.

"Well, afta-whiles they fin' it lit'l bunch ov gooses, an' that Coon he's tried that new way ketch 'em. Prit' soon he's got three ov it, jus' like he sed it. It's su'ah good ketch 'em that way. They jus' go on some mo' an' by-um-by seen it 'notha' lit'l bunches goose. He's swim it close to bank. Ol' Coon he sed it: 'Lit'l Couzzen, you like tried it this time? It's good chance.' So, lit'l fella' he's take that string an' he's go afta' it that gooses, an' prit' soon he's swim to bank jus' pullin three fat goose. He's jus' feel b-i-g, that lit'l fella, an Ol' Coon he's jus' glad fo' him too.

"So then, start home an' Ol' Coon sed it: 'To-morro' go' gen, lit'l fella', cause won't stay long now them goose, jus' go north. I come by you lodge when sun jus' pass middel, an' we go ketch 'em some mo' lots a gooses mebbe.'

"Nex' day Ol' Coon he's go down by that place what he sed it; but he ain't there, Lit'l Fox. He's wonda' what's matta lit'l fella, don' come. He's look prit' soon an' seen it that lit'l fella' jus' workin' hard in that garden-patches. Coon he's jus' whistle low like, an' that lit'l fella' he's heard it an' he's come down there where is it Ol Coon.

"Coon, he's sed it: 'Well, what's matta'? Le's go ketch 'em gooses 'gen.' That lit'l fella's he's jus' look sorrow, an' he's tell it, Ol' Coon, can't go, cause his uncle, it's come home. He say his uncle ask 'im how he's ketch it that gooses, an' when he tole him, he sed it why don' ketch 'em 'mo', he sed it his uncle: 'I could eat all of it that many myself.' Lit'l fella' sed it, 'I tole 'im go 'gen today, but uncle jus' say, he go he-self,' an' tole him lit'l fella' get long rope, stout one, bes' he could find, cause he's goin' try ketch 'em gooses, he-self. So lit'l fella' say he got 'im good rope fo' his uncle, an' that uncle he jus' went down to'wa'ds lake to tried it his lucks. He tole him, lit'l fella' to stayed home an' clear out 'notha' garden-patches. That Lit'l Fox he's jus' look sorrow, an' that Coon he's lis'n to him, an' jus' thinkin' lit'l bit.

"By-um-by they jus' heard it 'way down by lake, b-i-g squawk noise, an' lots a honk, honk, soun' like lots a auto'biles, I guess, jus soun' funny' like holla' lots a gooses. Jus' bofe stop talk an' lis'n. Seems like comin' close by, so that Coon an lit'l fella' jus' run top lit'l hill, it's close by, where could see betta' down on lake. It's look that way, an' could seen it b-i-g bunch gooses, jus' fly eva' which way an' down low, jus' make lots a squawkin' an' honk-honk noises. That Coon an' lit'l fella' jus' look at each otha', like say, what's matta'? Prit soon it's kin a strat'en out that bunch a goose, jus' fly mo' high up, an' then start out fly comin' this way. When it's come lit'l close, looks like they could seen it somethin' hang down, jus' swingin' like, unda' that bunch a gooses. Jus' comin close now, 'bout fly right ova' where it is that Coon an' Lit'l Fox. Then they seen it, what 'tis;

it's that Ol' Fox. That rope it's tie tight on his middel, an' it got lots goose foots tie on it too. He's jus' swingin', looks like ridin' good. When he's go by close, he's jus' holla' l-o-u-d, that Ol' Fox an' sed it: 'Nephew, took good care my garden-patches,' an' jus' keep right on ridin' f-a-s-t.

"Ol' Coon, he's try it not to smile an' he's say: 'Well, Lit'l Fella, I guess mebbe so, he tied it too much goose foots on his string, you uncle, he's got prit' good string seem like. It's new way travel, but I spec' he go long ways an' fin' it new place, mebbe so. I spec' not come back, long time, mebbe so betta' go some tell him, you aunt.'

"That Ol Fox he prit' smart, afta' all, I spec' mebbe so he's first one ride on airy-plane, ain't it?"

VII.

A PRE-HISTORIC RACE.

"Neh-ah, in the last story, Old Fox was certainly 'right up to date,' wasn't he? He had an aeroplane with a motor that couldn't go dead on him, and besides, he had a honk-honk that could scare everything out of the way. Now that there aren't any more stories about Old Fox and Old Coon, I wonder what you are going to tell me next. I'll read you some more of the 'Arabian Nights' and you can think up some others."

"Well, that good, but spec' betta' tole you 'notha' one tonight, cause jus' bin think 'bout it today, when you tole to me 'bout it that air-ship race, you read in noose-pay-pa'. That one 'mind me 'bout it, and jus' think it all ova' this afta'noon while I'm piecin' quilt.

"It's 'bout one o' you great-gran'fathas I 'spec,' 'cause you b'long to Big Turtle clan, jus' same as me and you' motha', an' our motha,' cause all a childrens have to b'long same clan as motha'. Long 'go, always bin lots a good chief an' warrior in Big Turtle clan. He's leader long 'go, way back, don' know how many hund'ed years. Lots ol' story tole 'bout it. Big Turtle he's hol' the world on his back fo' long time. Some day I tole you 'bout it.

"That Ol' Turtle, he's the one, he smart all a time. He jus' same since long time 'go, all a time know it what do. He can't scared him nobody, an' can't beat 'im nothin'. He's eva' time come out 'head.

"That why, long time 'go, Ol' Buffalo, he's eatin' 'roun' clos' edge of timber. He don't hungry, he's jus' bite ova here, ova' tha'. By-um-by he see Ol' Fox in bushes, he sed it: 'Yo-ho, my fren,' come ova' here, I like tell you this.'

"Ol' Fox he's lit'l smart too; he's crawl out trap e-a-s-y; he's hard to fin' it, too, sometime you hunt fo' him. He's jus' wonda' what's want Ol' Buffalo, an' what's got say; but he's come ova' tha', jus' jumpin' easy an' he's sed it: 'Well, my big fren', what you got say?'

"Ol' Buffalo, he says: 'My frien', I got

make race with Turtle. You kind a smart, an' you got sharp eyes, you be judge, see who beat 'em. You tell him, Ol' Turtle, I beat 'im on a groun' or in a wata', jus' how he like, I don' care nothin'. You tell 'im come tomorro' ova' there by lake when sun come up jus' 'bout high as sycamo' tree. You tell eva-body an' he can come see race. I be down tha', you tell 'im that, Ol' Turtle. He's always best one, eva' time; but I don't think he could run, it's too short his legs. Mebbe so he's run good in wata', tho'. Me too, I could run fas' in wata' or anyhow. I bet I could beat 'im'.

"Ol' Fox he say: 'I tell 'im Ol Turtle an' I tell 'im eva'body. I go now.' So he's go down by his lodge, Ol' Turtle, an' tell 'im all what he sed it, Ol' Buffalo.

"That Turtle, he's jus' lis'n an' don' say somethin' for long time. By-um-by he say: 'That's good, I run race on wata'. First one come to that island ova' there, he's the one what beat. You tell 'im, Ol' Buffalo, I be on han'. I don' say jus' what I'm do, but I do 'im. To-morro', when sun shine good, I come.'

"Fox, he's go back tell 'im, Ol' Buffalo, what say Ol' Turtle. All what he see on way, he tell 'em 'bout race. He sed it: 'You tell 'em eva-body, you tell 'em come.'

"Nex' day, ain't sun-up yet, Ol' Wolf he's go down by lake. He's make it fire, make smoke jus' go straight up, so can see eva'body, an' by-um-by, all come.

"Prit' soon he's come along, Ol' Turtle; jus' come slow an' go down clos' to edge wata'. He don' say nothin', jus' go slow, lookin' 'roun.' Buffalo an' Fox come too, an' bofe jus' talkin' all a time. Then come eva'body, Deer an' Bear, Coon, he come too. Turkey, Prai'chicken, Duck, an' Quail, Hawk he's tha' too, an' Little Turtle, Snipe, an' Ol' Beaver, Porkypine, Snake, an' Mud-Turtle; it's come eva'body I guess.

"While all jus' talk an' visit 'roun', Buffalo he's go down where Ol' Turtle he's settin' close to edge wata', he sed it: 'Well, my fren', you' legs prit' short, but I beat you this race, I think.' Turtle he don' say nothin', jus' lookin' 'cross lake to islan'. Buffalo sed it: 'You say we race on wata', I tell my fren' Fox be judge. It's high rock right ova' there, so Fox he's clim' up an' set down, an' he could jus' seen it, eva'thin'.

"Buffalo sed it: 'Well, it's re'dy. Wolf, you howl it, an' hit it three times queek on drum, an' we start.' Wolf, he say, 'Al'-right', an' he took he place. Prit soon he's howl, an' hit it three times on drum queek; they gone. Buffalo he's swim fast to'ads islan'. Turtle he jus' slip in wata', an' can't see him, nobody. He's go jus' like that wa'boat you tell it 'bout on otha' side Big Wata'; that Gemmany Keeza' summa-rine, unda' wata', an' when Buffalo jus' lit'l mo' 'an half-way, swimmin' fas', Ol' Turtle jus' crawl out slow on sho' of islan'. Eva'body looks funny, and Fox he's say: 'Turtle he's beat 'im.'

"Beaver' he's try it an' Turtle he's beat 'im. Nex' Deer he try; he's 'way behin' an' Turtle crawl out on islan'. Coon he's sed it: 'I sure can beat 'im, I re'dy now.' He's jus' got start, when Turtle crawl out on otha' side. Well, then Turkey say: 'I want beat 'im.' He can't do nothin'. Turtle he's right on islan' when Turkey he's come. Prai'chicken he say: 'I'm good racer, I could beat 'im'; but Turtle got tired waitin' for him on islan' befo' Prai'chicken got tha' an' start back. Quail, he's whist'l big, an' sed it: 'I'm the one could beat 'im Turtle.' Turtle neva' sed nothin', jus' get re'dy. They start an' befo' eva'body don' heard Quail, his wings any mo', Ol' Turtle he's crawl out on islan'.

"Fox, he's got tired sayin' 'Turtle's beat 'im'; so he said it: 'You can't do it, nobody. You can't beat 'im, Turtle. He's good racer in wata' cause he's all a time good swimma'. All what's got beat, mus' gif' to him somethin'.'

"Well, all them fellas what's got beat, Buffalo, Deer, Bear, Raccoon, Turkey, Prai'chicken, an' Quail, they jus' cut it off lit'l bit they own meat. They gif' to him, Turtle, jus' one piece to time. Turtle he's took it each lit'l bit when they gif' to him; don' sed nothin', jus' eat all of it.

"Then Fox he's sed it somethin', 'gen: 'Long as he live that Turtle, it be jus' same; if them peoples kill 'im an' roasted it or make 'em soup, it's tasted jus' like all a kinds game meats. Turtle, he's take it first place, at head all kin's animal. He wise an' brave, an' he don' all a time talk, he's do somethin'.'

"Turtle, he don' sed nothin'. Jus' ten' his own business, don't buck in nowhere. Don' botha' nobody. It was that way.

"But Turtle he's don' tell it them peoples that ol' Turtle, his brothah, look jus' like 'im, live on that islan'."

VIII.

THE EAGLE FEATHER.

"That race you told me about was a good story, Neh-ah, anyway that's what I think. Can't you think of another one about Old Turtle to go with it?"

"It's jus' all a time that way. I tole you one an' you jus' want it 'notha' one kin' a like it Some day it's goin' be all gone, story, what goin' do then?"

"Oh, let's don't think about that. I know you've got a whole lot of them yet, and if you do run out, why I'll just ask for some of the best ones, and you can tell them again. I never get tired of listening to any of them."

"Yooht—you jus' like that Ol' Turtle, he jus' get the best of 'im eva'body. Don' botha him nothin' an' he's just all a time go on an' 'ten to his own bizness. He don' worry 'bout it somethin', he's jus' think it out some way eva-time to come out 'head, an' he's do it too. I spec' that's why he's good leader, cause he jus' all a time lis'n, an' lookin' an' thinkin' fo' he-se'f.

"Well, I tole you 'bout eagle featha'. It's bes' kind like 'em, Injun. Long time 'go, can't wear it eva'body; womans, he don' wear 't all, an' young buck he couldn't wore it 'till he's do something big. Ol' time it's that way. Nowdays, jus' stick 'im in his hat, eagle featha' all a Injun, an' any body. Jus' same like that iron crosses what he's gif to all he so'jers, that Gemmenny Keeza', you read me 'bout 'em in paypa'.

"It's this way he's get it, eagle featha', first time, Injun. It's long 'go, jus' commence worl' I spec'. It's ol' man an' he nephew live togetha', jus' them two, it's all a people, them days. Ol' man he's jus' stay in lodge all a time. Young fella' he's go out get it, game, hunt. Well, one time come back lodge, don't get it nothin'. Uncle he's ask 'im what got, an' young fella' sed it: 'Nothin'.' Next day it's same way, an' jus' same way, 'notha times. It's three time, then when come back, young fella', an' his uncle sed it 'gen, that young fella' sed it: 'I pull it out eagle featha',' an' sure 'nough, he's got it that featha' in his hand. Ol' man he's jus' shook it, his head an' sed it: 'Oh, it's a big danger.'

"So he's tole young fella' hang it that featha' in smoke hole, top of lodge. He's do it, an' prit' soon they seen it that eagle fly slow like, ova' that smoke hole. He don' got that featha' tho'.

"Ol' man, he's sed it 'gen: 'That's a big danger, must call animals to Council. Musn't let get it, Eagle, that featha'.' So young fella' he's go tell 'em come to Council, 'bout that danger. By-um-by they all come; Big Turtle, Otter, Skunk, Porkypine, an' all of 'em. Ol' man tell 'em, 'We musn't let Eagle an' his fellas take it way from us that featha'.' He's pick out his crowd to hol' it that featha'. All them animal jus' talk heap 'bout what he can do. Some run fas', some could hide good, an' some could jus' make it big noise to scared it anything. Ol' man he's tol' Deer don't want 'im, cause can't run fas' 'nough. He don' want Wolf, he's too much howl, an' Bear cause he's too much all a time sleep it.

"He's pick it out Big Turtle, Porkypine, an' some mo' fo' he side. Prit' soon they seen it, Eagle jus' fly low ova' smoke hole, 'gen. Some them fellas what he don' take it, Ol' Man fo' his side, jus' get mad to him, an' sed it: 'We goin' he'p it, Eagle.'

"Turtle, he's slip 'roun' an' got it that

THE EAGLE FEATHER

featha', an' tole it his men: 'Le's go.' They start off lit'l ways an' come to big tree. Turtle sed it: 'Le's clim' up.' So all of 'em clim' tree. They look 'way off an' seen it comin' Eagle. Jus' 'bout that time it's come big wind. It's rotten that tree, an' jus' broke it an' fall down. They jus' go eva' which way, all them fellas. Porkypine, he's all cover up with rotten wood, but he's chawed it 'way an' crawl out. Mebbe so that's why he's all a time like to chawed it rotten woods, Porkypine. An' he's kin' a hurt too, lit'l bit, Porkypine, so, when Turtle say: 'Le's go, hurry,' Porkypine say he can't travel. Then he's tole 'im Turtle, 'Get on my back, an' he's give him basket ashes to scatta' on his tracks, that Turtle, so can't fin' trail, nobody, them otha fellas.

"He's got it that featha', Turtle. Well, it's started all of 'em. Turtle Porkypine on he back, they las' one. Porkypine he's jus' get it busy scatta' ashes on Turtle, his tracks; but shucks, it don't hide 'em track 't 'all, jus' make easy to see it trail.

"They jus' go on hurry, an'way, an' it's prit' nea' get to riva', when he's heard 'em comin, Eagle an' his bunch. Jus' 'bout edge of wata', Turtle, an' they jus' holla, 'Who-o!' an' jump out an' ketch 'em that Turtle, Eagle, his bunch. They try to take it 'way Turtle, that featha'; but can't do it. Turtle got it in he mouth an' can't let it go, an' won't give up, that Turtle, e'tha'.

"So he sed it, them fellas: 'We fix it, Ol' Turtle.' An' one of it jus' mek it fire an' when it's burn good, they jus' pick 'im up Turtle an' carry 'im bottom side up top, an' jus' hol' him ova' fire. Ol' Turtle sed it: 'Oh that such a nice, I jus' like it that kind, plenty hot, don't took me out a fire my fren's, I like it.' Them fellas jus' mad an' sed it: 'It don't hurt 'im fire, le's took 'im out, whip 'im.' So they take it out fire, an' some fellas get good sticks an' jus' beat 'im, Turtle, on his back. Turtle jus' commence sing, jus' like it was beatin' drum, them fellas, an' jus' seem like a happy. He's mad some mo' them fellas, an' Turtle he's got it yet that featha'.

"Somebody sed it: 'Le's throw 'im in riva'.' So they pick him up an' start do that. That Turtle he's jus' scream, an sed it he's 'fraid a wata' an' 'jus' beg 'em not put 'im in riva'. He's jus' push back an' holla' an' don't want go 'tall, jus' mek 'em big fuss. Them fellas jus' glad then to heard 'im, an' sed it: 'We jus' throw it in deepes' wata' we could find.' An' sure 'nough they jus' pitch 'im that Turtle, 'way out in deep wata', ka-zowey. They could seen him sink down bottom of riva' an' layin' on his back, like dead, but he's got that featha, yet.

"Well, them otha' fellas think its dead, Turtle; but prit' soon they seen 'im swim out 'cross riva' an' clim' up on big log,

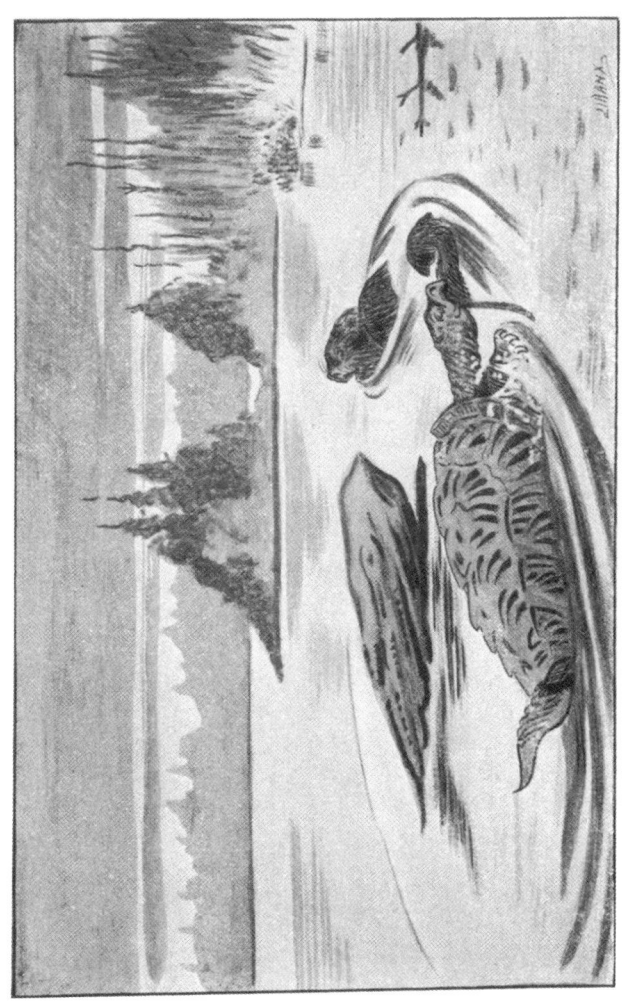

THE EAGLE FEATHER

an' he's jus' wave that eagle featha' an' jus' give big wah-whoops.

"So, them fellas hold council, an' they sed it: 'Somebody mus' go get it, that featha'; but don't want go nobody, cause 'fraid of wata.' By-um-by talk some mo', an' send it, Otter. He's swim out that log quick, an' Turtle, he's jus' set there an' hol' it up that featha'. 'Bout time Otter he's get there, an' goin' crawl on that log, Turtle, he's drop in wata' on otha' side log. He's go unda' log prit' quick on otha' side, 'gen, an' he's bite on end Otter his tail. Then jus' go 'roun' an' 'roun' that log Otter an' Turtle. That Otter he's jus' holla'; 'Ow-we-e, he's hurt me, ow-we-e!' Prit' soon that Turtle, he's bite off piece tail an' Otter, he's get 'way, hurry, an' swim to sho'.

"Turtle, he's get on log 'gen an' wave that eagle featha' an' jus' whoop 'em heap.

"They couldn't beat 'im nobody, that Turtle, that's cause he's bes' one yet."

IX.

WHY AUTUMN LEAVES ARE RED.

A WYANDOT MYTH.

It had been a clear winter's day, not cold and with just enough bright sunshine on the first light snow that had fallen. The boy had been out in the woods with his dog; and down in a sheltered place along the bluffs, he found some dog-wood shoots yet bearing their brillantly colored leaves. Gathering some of these he had brought them home and placed them in an old silver flagon that stood on the mantel-piece. They made a wonderful bit of bright, cheery color in the room.

Of course he called his Aunt's attention to them, for he well knew how much she liked bits of bright color.

He saw her look thoughtfully at their scarlet and crimson and was all interest, yet not surprised when she said:

"Ol' Ouendots use's tell story 'bout how come leaves get prit' color in fall times. Not long one, story, but jus' kin' a nice. Cou'se it's 'bout some animals, cause seems like long time 'go they was live first, 'fo' peoples. They somethin' like peoples, too, I guess, cause they do so much things all a same like.

"Didn't I ever tol' you what's reason it's red an' color, all tree leafs in fall time?

"Well, it's like this one: Long 'go when

it's all fix it up, Sky-land, by Little Turtle, Deer, he's got in hurry an' went up tha' 'fore it's all fix it fo' animals. It's jus' mek 'em mad, all of 'em, cause that Deer he's all a time such hurry to buck in.

"Afta' while when it's all ready eva-thing, Bear, it's his time to go up tha', so he's go up by that nice road what he's fix it, Little Turtle, an' when he's got up tha' prit' soon, he's meet 'im, Deer. He's sed to him: 'What fo' you come here so hurry, 'fo' he's tol' you, Little Turtle, it's ready?' Deer, he's awfu' proud like' an' he's jus' shook his head, an' sed it: 'Nobody but Wolf could ask that to me, he's the one to sed it, not you.' An' by-um-by, he's sed it, 'notha' 'gen: 'I'll jus' give you whippin', Bear, cause you such a smart,' an' that Deer his eyes jus' like fire, an' hair on his back, jus' stan' up straight cause he's mad.

"Bear, cause can' 'fraid him nothin', he's jus' stan' tha' waitin' fo' that Deer to jump on him, I spec'.

"Then Deer start it. Bear jus' growl big, mek loud noise, jus' like shake sky, an' he sharp claw jus' tear that Deer, an' Deer, his sharp horn an' foot, jus' cut that Bear. They fight long time an' mek big noise. They could heard it them otha's down on Great Island. Then they sent him up that Wolf to stop it that fight.

"Wolf, he's get up tha' an' he's got hard time to mek stop it that big fight, that Deer an' Bear; but he's do it prit' soon, an when

that Deer, he's run 'way, his horn jus' all drippin' with blood, that Bear's. That blood jus' fall down on tree leafs on Great Island, an' mek it all red color. It's that way yet, ev' time come 'roun' that time they fight it, that Deer an' that Bear, leafs jus' get that way, red.

"They sed it long 'go, Ol' Ouendots."

X.

THE FERRYMAN.

When this story was finished, the old clock hadn't yet, as Neh-ah sometimes remarked: "He's sed it, eight."

The Boy was ready with another suggestion, and said: "Now Neh-ah, you've told me such a good story about the red leaves, I think you'll have to tell another about a rabbit. Old Jolly and I brought home seven. You'd hardly believe it, but Jolly run one into a b-i-g hollow red-oak that stands down on the hill-side. Some-one had cut a hole in one side of it and I crawled in; and down in the old hollow roots running all 'round, I kept pulling out rabbits until I had seven. Mebbe we won't have a pot-pie, and I'll sell some of them in town, too."

Neh-ah listened smilingly to the Boy, then said: "Well, guess can't cross riva' no mo' nobody, cause must be you kill all the ferrymans. You don't give 'im no good chance or mebbe so they foolish you like he done to one fella, one time.

"I didn't tell you befo' 'bout Rabbit, is it? He's live long time 'go down on riva', an' he's got good canoe, an' jus' took 'em eva-body cross riva', like what you call it ferry-boat, aint it?

"Well, one time Rabbit, he's sittin' down on riva' bank, jus' singin' an' waitin' like, an' prit' soon he's holla' somebody, otha' side of riva. Rabbit, he's look and seen it, Ol' Wolf, so he's jus' don' mek no 'tention, jus' keep on singin' like don't heard nothin'. That Wolf, he's mean one, all a time want kill 'em somebody, an' Rabbit he don't like 'em.

"Prit' soon Wolf sed it: 'Hey, you fella' you feet it's crooked out, come took me 'cross riva'.'

Rabbit, he's jus' ke'p on singin', an' by-um-by he's say: "Long 'go, I all a time dance plenty at feast, 'at's why it's crooked out, my foots."

"Wolf sed it: 'Hey, you fella, 'at's got l-o-n-g ears, jus' stick it up straight, come took me 'cross riva'.'

"Rabbit, he say: 'My ears stick it up, 'cause long 'go I could wear many eagle featha', ain't it?'

"Wolf, he sed it: 'Hey, you fella', it's split you lip, come take a me ova' riva'.'

"Rabbit, he say: 'It's that way my lip, cause long 'go, I whistle much at big dance, ain't it?'

"Wolf, he's jus' mad now, and' sed it: 'Oh, you jus' brag heap, all a time, I get you now.' Then he's jus' jump in riva' an' swim 'cross. Rabbit he's run an' Wolf he's took afta' him. He's run long ways an' jus' gettin' tired, but Wolf, he's comin', he's prit' close now. Rabbit, he's come to hollow tree, an' he's jump in hole, jus' time Wolf he's goin' ketch 'im.

"Wolf, he's mad, an' he jus' goin' stand by that hole till that Rabbit, he's come out, n'en he ketch 'em sure, so he's stay right tha'. Rabbit he's rest lit'l time, n'en he's go out notha' hole an' go back to his canoe. L-o-n-g time afta' Wolf, he's get heap tired that what you call it, watch-ful-a-waitin', an' he's go back down riva'. He's look otha' side an' seen it that Rabbit sit on his canoe, jus' like bin tha' all a time.

"That's time he don' ketch 'im Rabbit, that Ol' Wolf, ain't it?"

XI.

OLD COON TEACHES THE WOLF TO HUNT.

Neh-ah and the Boy were sitting just in the fire light one night when the old woman said:

"You jus' always like it to hear 'em so much story 'bout Ol' Fox an' Ol' Coon, I jus' happen today, think of 'notha' one kin' a like it. 'Tain't Ol' Fox tho', cause he's gone an' I don' eva' hear if he's come back. Mebbe so if you heard it some day 'bout his come back, you could tell that story. But that Ol' Coon he jus' always took eva' chance what come 'long to play trick on somebody.

"Any-how, I tole you this story jus' same way you Uncl' Jim Clark use' tole it long 'go in Canada. He was good one to tole story, only some-time he jus' put in lots a cuss words like he all a time sed it whitemans. Them Injun boy long time 'go 'at's jus' first thing learn Inglis', it's the cuss words. I guess it's cause in Injun langwige they don' got none, cuss words.

"It's long time afta' he's gone that Fox, one day Ol' Wolf he's prowlin' 'long riva' an' he's meet 'im that Coon. Ol' Coon he's bin on visit 'way out west to pra'rie peoples, an' he's bring it home big bundl' buffalo meat. He's jus' eatin' piece when he's come 'long Ol' Wolf.

"Wolf he's sed it: 'Hello, my Couzzen, what kin' meats you eat 'em, an' where you get it? I don' had no good meats fo' long time, it's kin' a sca'ce now days, ain't it?'

"Ol' Coon he's jus' kin' a grin, an' gif to him piece of meat, that Wolf, an' he's sed it: 'Oh, it's a buffalo meats what I got. I ketch 'em that kin' buffalo out on pra'rie, where I bin few day. It's lots of it there, buffalo, an' it's kin easy to ketch 'em that kin' too.'

"Wolf, he's jus' eatin' an' it's sure taste good that meats. Prit' soon he's say: 'How you sed it's easy to ketch it that kin'? He's big' one than you are, an' could run fas'. I don' see how you mek it easy to ketch 'em that kin'.'

"'Well,' Coon sed it, 'I could tole you

how it's easy ketch'em, you wants to tried it. He's big one, but he's easy to 'fraid, an' when he's heap 'fraid, he's jus' scare to death, jus' run 'til it's kill himsel'.'

"Wolf he's say: 'You ketch 'im that way?'

"'Yes, I ketch 'im,' he sed it Coon. I jus' tole you all 'bout it an' you could tried it an' ketch 'em good, then you have lots a good meats. You could start fo' prai'rie pri't soon an' come to edge, long 'bout dark come, jus' befo'. You jus' look 'roun' good an' fin' it bunch buffalo, eat 'roun' close to bushes. You watch 'em 'n' afta' whiles its tired eat it, an it's lay down sleep it. When he's good lay down sleep it, you jus' go 'long easy, slip up behin' an' you jus' tied it, that buffalo, his tail 'roun you-sel', you middel. It's long hair on his tail, that fella'. You mus' tied it good, so can't slip off, cause if slip off, he's turn 'roun' jus' step on you, sure. When get it tie up good, you jus' mek big noise—whoo, whoo. Buffalo he's so scare he's jump up an' run, an' you jus' took good ride, cause you jus' go with 'im, an' jus' all a time go whoo, whoo. That buffalo he jus' run heap, he's so scare, an' prit' soon he's jus' drop dead, then you mus' cut it, his throat, an' you got heap good eat.'

"Wolf, he's jus' lis'n, an' he's sed it:

"'It's soun' good, I guess mebbe so, I tried it. Le's go, you jus' watch a me, I kill 'em buffalo.'

"So Coon he's go long, an' they start it

for pra'rie. It's 'bout dark when they gets to edge of timber, an' right clos' by seen it bunch buffalo. Wolf an' Coon jus' lay down rest lit'l bit, an' watch it that buffalo. Afta' while it's got 'nuff eat it, an' jus' all laid down to sleep it.

"Wolf, he's jus' feelin' prit' good an' he's pick it out big fat, she one buffalo. Well, when he's sleep it good that ol' she one, buffalo, Coon tell him betta' go now, an' he's slip out easy an' he's tied he-se'f good to that she one, buffalo, his tail, an' when it's all tie up tight, Wolf, he's jus' go holler: 'Whoo, whoo.' That she one, buffalo, he's 'fraid plenty. He jus' jump up an' holler: 'Bra-a-h, bra-a-h,' an' jus' go run, he so scare, jus' like what's say white peoples:

'scare like hell.' He sure run fas' an' that Wolf he's jus' hol' tight on his tail, that she one, buffalo, an' jus' ride fas' too. Eva' once while, buffalo jus' kick 'im in ribs an' Ol' Wolf he's go up in air. Prit' soon he's gone out a sight, buffalo an' wolf. Ol' Coon he's jus' kin' a chuckle an' sed it to he-self: 'I guess mebbe so, my couzzen, he's get prit' good ride, now, won't get back fo' many moons, mebbe so, spec' he's go 'long ways.'

"But that Wolf, he don' ride such long time, cause that she one, buffalo, he's come to big mud hole, wide one, an' jus' 'bout time he's get middel that mud hole, he's mek big kick an' that Wolf, he's break it loose from tail, jus' go up in air, an' come down tchi-wash in that sof' muds. He's kin' a glad too, cause don' want it no buffalo meats now. He's crawl out mud hole kin' slow, cause prit' sore, an' start off kin' a limp, an' he sed it to he-self: 'That Coon he's don' say how long got to ride it, that buffalo. I guess he's jus' mek it foolish with me. Nex' time I don't tried it what he say.

It's jus' same kin' he's always foolish 'im that Ol' Fox. He's bad rascal that Coon.

XII.

THE HOLE IN THE SKY

OR

HOW THE SUMMER BECAME LONGER.

"Well, I guess that Old Coon never did stop playing his pranks. I only wish that more of his tricks had been told in other stories, for it is sure fun to listen to them." So the Boy said one evening when he was not quite sure that Neh-ah had another story for him. He was right pleasantly surprised when she at once said:

"I goin' tell you 'notha one Uncle Jim's story. Ol' Tah-too-tahn-yoh, he's ol' 'Jibway man what's marry to Ouendot woman, an live 'mongst our people in Canada, long 'go. Lots a boys jus' go down his house winta' time an' he's tell 'em ol' story, sometimes prit near all night. They jus' pitch in an' cut it lots wood fo' ol' man an' he's tell 'em ol' story. It's good story, this one, I like it my-se'f.

"Long time 'go, ol' people use tole 'bout it, it's jus' col' all a time, prit' near. I think mebbe so, it's that time, t'aint very ol' world, cause it's them days, peoples and animals, jus' kin' a all a same like, sometimes they be peoples, sometimes some kin' animal, jus' what kin' they like. They know how to do eva-thing them days, got power, jus' like what call white peoples now, witch, I guess, anyhow, could do jus' what want do, anything.

"Well, it's them days, good hunta', he's lodge not far from Big Watah; but it's nobody live clos' by, jus' him an' woman, an' got one boy, lit'l fella, jus' 'bout half way grown to man. It's big country, lots tree, big ones all 'run' where he's live, that huntah. He's got strong power, could prit' near do it anything. Sometime he's man, an' sometime he's that lit'l kin' animal what dey call it, Fisher, jus' kin'a like that Otter, 'at's his Couzzen, an' kin' a looks like 'im, but he ain't that big. That Ol' Otter, he's kin' a funny fella, he's jus' all a time, laff an' sing, an' have good fun. He's all a time talk heap, too; but he don' sed nothin' much, jus' talk. He's good fella, tho, an' jus' try to do it anything what tell 'im, somebody.

"That hunta' he's all a time kill 'em heap deer, an' eva' kin' a game, so, jus' have plenty to eat. That woman, he's good one, too, jus' take care that game what he's kill 'em, dried that deer meat an' smoke 'im, an' mek that fine buck-skin fo' moccasin an' leggins.

"They jus' like 'im, heap, that lit'l fella' too. That hunta' he's mek 'im good lit'l bow an' arrows, an' showed 'im how hunt bird an' squirrels; an' that woman, he's mek 'em lit'l moccasins an' leggin' an' huntin' shirt. Snow shoes too, cause it's jus' plenty snow that country all a time. It's that way them days, jus' col' an' snow prit' near all time.

"That lit'l fella' he's jus' go hunt by himse'f an' bring 'em back to lodge, bird an' squirrels; but he's jus' get prit' near freeze it eva' time. His finger jus' 'bout freeze it, an' can't shoot good, an' sometime jus' mek 'im mad, an jus' cried, cause it so cold, don' know what do. He's jus' wish it don' be so much freeze it an' cold fo' so many days.

"Well, one time, that lit'l fella', he's bin hunt, an' jus' comin' back to lodge. Oh, it's col', an' that lit'l fella', he's 'bout froze it now. He's comin' 'long, an' he's seen it, squirrel, it's sit on bush lit'l way head, it's eatin' somthin'. He's wonda' that lit'l fella' why don' run, squirrel, an' he's jus' fix it his arrow to shoot it. 'Bout that time, that squirrel, he sed it:

"Grandson, musn't shoot it, me. Put it down you bow cause I got somethin' to sed to you. You jus' lis'n an' you do what I sed it. Long time I seen it you don't like it heap col' an' snow, I seen you huntin' an' jus' can't help it, cry some time, cause heap col'. It's too plenty col' all a time, anyhow, I don' like it too. Now I tole you what do, an' we fix it mo' summa' time. You fatha', he's strong power, he could do it prit' near anything. When you get you lodge, you mus' jus' cryin' all a time. Yo' motha', he's want know what's matta', you jus' don' sed nothin', jus' cryin', an' cryin' heap. Jus' keep it cryin' all a time 'til he's come, you fatha'; then when he's ask it what's matta' don' sed nothin' fo' long time, but jus' cryin' an' cryin' jus' likes feel so bad, can't sed nothin'. Then afta' whiles, you tell 'im: 'Me, I don't like it too much col' all a time, I jus' want mo' summa' times.' Just sed it: 'Oh, my fatha' can't you have him, somebody, make it mo' summa' times, an' **don'** have it so much col' an' snows. Oh, I don' like it so much col'.'

"So, that lit'l fella, he tole 'im, squirrel, he do that way, an' he's got to lodge, he's jus' cryin' an' cryin', jus' like it hurt somethin' but don' know what. He motha' ask it what's matta', but jus' shook head **an'** don't sed it nothin', jus' push 'way what's want 'im to eat it, his motha', an' jus' keep cryin' 'til it's come his fatha', then he's **do** jus' like what's tole 'im that squirrel.

"Well, he fatha' sed it: 'My son, I try do that what you sed it. It's much hard thing to do, but I tried, cause my son want it that kin'.' So that lit'l fella' he's stop it cryin' an' eat it what gif to 'im his motha'. That Fisher sed it, he mus' make feast an' call council for his frens'. Nex' day they cook it whole bear, an' sen' word to Otter, Beaver, Lynx an' Badger to come that feast an' council. Well, afta' whiles, it's come eva'body an' had it big eats; then all a them fella' jus' sit 'round an' prit' soon smoke it peace-pipe, then jus' talk 'bout it, what's got do.

"Afta' talk 'bout it long time, all them otha' fellas' sed it they go with that Fisher an' he'p 'im. He sed it, they go in three days. Time come that Fisher he tole it goodby, that woman, an' lit'l fella', an' he's jus' feel heap bad, cause he's know mebbe so he don' seen it no mo'.

"Then he's start all of it, an' jus' go on, don't meet 'im nothin' 'til 'bout twenty days, it's come to foot of high mountain. Jus' could look up as want to, an' can't see it top, it's h-i-g-h, that mountain. They fin' it tracks, like kill it somethin', somebody, jus' while 'go; you could see bloody, an' that track goin' up mountain. That Fisher he sed it, 'betta' follow it that track, mebbe-so fin' it somethin' eat it.' So, jus' followed it, track, an' prit' soon, come to lodge. Fisher, he tole 'em, mus' be still, don' laugh 't'all.

"By-um-by, they saw ol' man stan' in

door that lodge. He's jus' crooked eva' which way, jus' all twist up. He's got b-i-g head, an' funny kin' teetch, jus' all stick out an' he don't had no arms. Them fella's they wonda' how he could kill 'em anything. That ol' man he's ask 'em come in his lodge, cause it's jus' 'bout night, come.

"That ol' man, he's strong Monedo, he could do anything. Well, afta' whiles ol' man he's bring out big bowl meat, an' he's jus' gif to them fellas' some fo' their suppa'. He's jus' move 'roun' heap funny, an that Otter, he jus' can't he'p it, an' prit soon he's laugh. That Monedo, he's jus look at 'im, an' jus' jump on him goin' smother 'im, cause it's that way he's kill it anything. But that Otter, when he's felt ol' crooked man light on he's head, he's jus' slip out from unda' 'im an' he's jus' run out door an' get 'way; but that Monedo he's sed it bad fo' 'im that Otter.

"Rest of 'em they eat, an' smoke an' talk, prit' near all night. That ol' man he's tole Fisher he could do what's he's want do; but it's a hard one to do, an' mebbe so, it's kill 'im. He's tole 'im which way to go, an' sed it fo' them to do like he said it, an' if follow that road, it sure take 'em right place. Whe' he's tole 'em all 'bout jus' what to do it, eva'- body sleep it lit'l time.

"Come nex' mornin', started go on. Jus' gone lit'l ways an' meet it tha' Otter, he's 'bout freeze it, an' kin' a hungry; but that Fisher, he's took 'long some that meat what's gif to 'im that ol' crooked man, so that Otter he's eat it. He don' laff this time.

"Well' jus' travel eva' day 'till it's bout twenty days 'gen, an' they come to that place what's tell 'em 'bout, that Monedo. It's the highest mountain, yet. Have to clim' long ways 'fo' get to top, but they get up tha' an' jus sit down rest and smoke it,' peace-pipe, cause got to do that kin ask 'em Great Spirit, he'p 'em. Jus' put it tobacco in that pipe, an' hol' it up to sky, then to no'th, an' east, an' south, an' west, then to earth then smoke it. It's so high up that mountain, that looks like sky right tha', an' think, an' look all 'roun' fo' long time, an' afta' whiles, that Fisher, he sed it, 'We mus' get ready,' an' he's tell 'em, 'We got to mek hole in sky.' He's tole it that Otter try it first. Jus' jump up 'gainst it hard as you can, mebbe so break it hole. Otter, he's jus' kin' a laff, an' sed it, 'I tried it, mebbe so.' He's jus' jump hard, jus' hit that sky so hard it's jus' bounce 'im back, an' prit' near knock stuffin' out that Otter. He's fall on snow right on he's back, an' it's kin' slick that snow, an' that Ol' Otter he's jus' go slidin' like eva'thing, clear to bottom that mountain. I bet he's neva' travel that fas' 'gen. When he's come to bottom, he's shake he-se', an' sed it, 'I think mebbe so, I gone home, I don' like make it that jump 'notha' 'gen,' so he's jus' pull it out fo' home.

"Well, that Beaver, he's tried it, an' it's fall down all a sense knock it out that fella'.

Then Lynx, he's tried it an' it's jus' all a f-a-r, an' it's plenty grass, plenty tree, same kin', jus' laid tha' like's dead.

"'Now,' he sed it, Fisher, to Badger, 'You tried it, it's strong, you people an' could do heap.'

"Badger he's jus' tried hard, an' it's knock 'im back that sky, but don' hurt 'im, so, he's jus' jump up an' he's tried it 'notha' 'gen. This time, its look's kin' a like it's crack, that sky, so Badger, he's jus' puff up b-i-g, an' he's jump, like a white peoples sed it: 'jus' like a hell.' It's bust hole in sky an' Badger he's go through an' that Fisher, he's jus' jump in right afta' 'im.

"Them two fellas' jus' look 'roun' an' oh, it's fin' place, jus' like a prai'e, could see plenty all kin's flower. Jus' litl' stream run eva' which way, lots a birds jus' ever kin' prit' ones jus' singin' eva' direction, oh it's jus' like a nice eva'where. Right ova' tha' they seen it some good ones' lodges an' way ova' good ways off could seen it lots a peoples jus' playin' ball, havin' good time.

"Don't seen nobody in them lodges but could see lots mo-cocks an' baskets an' it's all jus' full all kin' birds, prit' ones. That Fisher he's jus' think of that lit'l fella' an' they jus' cut it open them mo-cocks an' baskets all they could an' let it out all those kin' birds an' all of it jus' go big bunch an' fly down that hole in sky what's made it Badger. An' all that warm weather what's 'roun' tha' it's go down that hole too, an' jus' spread out all 'roun'. Prit' soon them peoples way ova' tha' they see it them fellas' what's doin' an' jus' come run ova' that way; but time they get ova' tha' it's 'bout all gone through that hole, all a summa' time weather, jus' 'bout lef' nothin' cep' its tail, an' one fella's he's come runnin', an' he's hit it with big club, an jus' broke it off tail; summa' time 'bout to went through that hole.

"That Badger, when he's seen 'em comin' them fellas' he's jus' run fo' that hole but that Fisher, he's jus' keep on lettin' out lots mo' bird fo' that lit'l fella', an' he's stay too long, that hole it's growed up an' can't get through. Well, he's jus' strike out runnin' cause to get 'way from them otha' fellas,' an' he's run fas'. Prit' soon he's come

to tall tree an' he's clim' up. They come,
them fellas', an' shoot at 'im, arrows; but
that fella you couldn't hurt 'im if you hit
'im, jus' one place arrow could hurt 'im, jus'
'bout one inch end of he's tail. Prit' soon
one arrow hit 'im on that place. It's prit'
bad. He's look down tha' an' seen it one
them fellas', he's got totem same like what
he's got. So, he's holla to him, this fella',
an' he's tole 'im, 'you my couzzen, tell 'em
don' kill me.' When dark come them fellas'
quit shoot, an' that Fisher, he's come down.
he's feel prit' bad, cause it's bleed heap. So
he's start crawl 'long to north, mebbe so he
fin' hole in sky he can go through; but he's
jus' keep travel 'til he's 'bout give out, don'
fin' none. So, he's stretch out his legs, his

head to no'th, an sed it: 'Well, I did that what's want, lit'l fella. It's make it betta' fo' all of its peoples, have mo' summa' times now, maybe eight o' nine moons, summa' time, then he's jus' die. Them fellas' fin' it nex' day, stretch it out dead. You could see it in sky now, it's tha' yet. While peoples call it that stars, Big Bear."